U0164519

01. DJ Play My Favorite Song
02. Original Colour
03. Erotica
04. Missing Of A Pair Of Converse
05. (Three Instruments) Of Peace
06. Going Separate Ways
07. Toys
08. Don' t Like Those Who Smoke Cigarettes
09. Lucky Star
10. NMN
11. Wars
12. Confession Of A Mistress
13. Rain
14. AML
15. Child
16. Humans Are Sad After Lovemaking
17. Kaleidoscope
18. Let Go Of The One You Love
19. AI
20. 3 Minute Summons
21. If Sydney Had A Disneyland
22. Life Journey Theory
23. Award Ceremony
24. Meeting Love At Eslite Bookstore In Taipei
25. Free Me
26. Hong Kong
27. Young Is Innocent
28. Bid Farewell To The Material   Going To The Soul
29. Bitch I Am Gawan!

我不在乎別人怎麼樣看我
也不刻意討好他人而墮落
我知道做什麼
我知道為什麼
當我失敗時痛苦承受那結果
當我灰心時宣洩情緒後好過
計較又會如何
時間一樣走過

為了誰　　為了我
選擇不了麼

DJ play my favorite song
我感動淚流下不多
儘管外寒冷　　冷雨下雪
在此我感覺溫暖火焰烈
DJ play my favorite song
把昔日經歷珍藏著
我有力量去　　抵擋那負面
努力去改變成為發亮的我

每段時間留下獨有痕跡
歡欣滿載亦有眾低潮
心靈伴侶是
內心那個自己
不嫌少　　不嫌
只是得一個

DJ play my favorite song
安慰我內心的沈默
我不凍不寒　　但身心似火
熱情去面對一切的結果
DJ play my favorite song
不理會他人做什麼
做我所做的　　做你所做的
沒有矛盾衝突敵對方
不需妒忌一切的結果
不需盼望他有的結果
杜絕夜長夢多紛擾我
杜絕自卑感覺傷害我

DJ play my favorite song
我已準備好了　　四射那艷光

DJ play my favorite song
淡然去看待是非錯
我不是聖賢　　也不是神明
不知道將來是福是禍
DJ play my favorite song
我歡樂地隨聲唱和
充滿正能力　　自信安全感
完整的我準備發亮發光

我只想喚回那快樂的我　　(DJ play my favorite song)
這首歌重要每年提點我　　（我歡樂地隨聲唱和）
自我感覺不需你告訴我　　（我不凍不寒　　但身心似火）
這份禮物都可屬於你

01.　DJ Play My Favorite Song

I don't care what others think of me
Don't deliberately please others and fall into disgrace
I know what to do
I know why
When I fail I suffer the consequences
When I feel discourage I feel better after letting my emotions out
What will happen if I care about it
Time passes by the same way

For whom   For me
Can't I choose

DJ play my favorite song
I was moved and shed few tears
Even though it's cold outside
It's raining coldly and snowing
I feel warm and burning here
DJ play my favorite song
Treasure the past experiences
I have the strength
To resist that negativity
Try to change and become a brighter me

Each time leaves unique traces
Full of joy but also many lows
Soulmate is
The self inside
Not too few   Not too
Just have one

DJ play my favorite song
Comfort the silence in my heart
I'm neither cool nor cold
But my body and mind are on fire
Face all consequences with enthusiasm
DJ play my favorite song
Ignore what others do
Do what I do   Do what you do
No conflict or fight between opposing parties
No need to be jealous of all results
No need to hope for the result he will have
Prevent long nights of dreams from disturbing me
Stop feeling inferior and hurt me

DJ play my favorite song
I'm ready to shine that bright light

DJ play my favorite song
Look at right and wrong indifferently
I'm not a sage   Or a god
I don't know whether the future will be a blessing or a curse
DJ play my favorite song
I sing along happily
Full of positive abilities   Self-confidence and security
I am complete and ready to shine

I just want to bring back the happy me
(DJ play my favorite song)
This song reminds me every year
(I sing along happily)
You don't need to tell me how I feel about myself
(I'm neither cool nor cold, but my body and mind are on fire)
This gift can be yours

01. DJ Play My Favorite Song

你的顏色
不用遮掩你真實的原色
是漂亮的
世界　　的流言
由它不許影響你的與生俱來的本質
不許放棄

你的彩虹顏色照耀著
我引以自豪的
你追求的方向
不是墮落自卑
別浪費精力
愛你的原色　　你的原色
使生命更亮醉

藍色的你
向我微笑但我是明白的
需要勇氣
縱使別人看不起你咒你罵你傷害了你
我永遠都靠站在你　　替你打氣
彩紅是七色的　　為什麼
呈現不同的特質　　是包容的標誌
不能去逃避　　是天意
是自由顏色　　愛的顏色
隨它存在　　很美

Oh. . . . La. . . .

（不要放棄　　我為你而驕傲）

如果世界迫得大緊
無法藏身自處
我會毫不介意給你安身之處

請保留你的原色　　不需怯
不要刻意去躲避　　你獨有的魅力
眾說錯是錯
繼續發亮
你的彩虹顏色　　你的原色
最美原色永恆註
就當世界瘋了
是一條不歸路
由它自我摧毀
不屑一眼走你的路
去追求　　自由的愛
原色不孤獨
是最美

02. 原色

Your colour
No need to hide your original colour
Is beautiful
World's rumour
Let it go and disallow it to affect your inherent nature
Can't give up

Your rainbow's colour is shining
I am proud of it
Your direction of pursuit
Is not deprave and inferior
Don't waste your energy
Love your original colour   Your original colour
Making life to be more shining and drunken

You are blue
Smiling at me but I understand
Need to have courage
Notwithstanding that you are
—being looked down cruse condemned harmed
I will stand by you forever   Cheer for you
Rainbow has seven colours   Why
Presenting different characters   Is a sign of tolerance
Cannot avoid   Is the meaning of sky
Is the colour of freedom   Colour of Love
Let it exists   Is beautiful

Oh....La....

(Don't give up   I am proud of you)

If the world presses on you so hard
No way to hide
I do not mind and will let you have a safe home

Please reserve your original colour   No need to afraid
Do not escape deliberately   Your unique charisma

It is wrong for other's stated fault
Keeping on shining
Your colour of rainbow
Your original colour
The everlasting existence of
—your most beautiful original colour
Assuming the world is crazy
Is a road of no end
Let it be self-destructed
No sight on what road you are walking
To pursue   Freedom of love
Original colour is not lonely
Is the most beautiful

02. Original Colour

惡魔是沒有形式和性別，
並藏在每個人的內心。

An evil has no form and gender
and hides inside everyone's
heart.

情慾
浪漫
情慾
激情

我不是情婦　　也不是你的午夜午郎
今晚由我來負責調教
將你由頭到尾切換
將我灌輸入你腦海然後進入體內
你會不能自拔嗎
由我來主導你應該走的方向
不需要拘緊自己
由我的手和口遊走

咀停留或是前進
進入胸膛然後去哪裡
愛感覺停留　　　暖入禁區的入口
你不需動　　由我來按開關制
你本能反應　　　已將一切赤裸
喔喔喔喔
我要進入你森林的盡頭
及河流

情慾　　情慾
從你身體各處找入口
情慾　　情慾
從我身體各處找出口
情慾
刺激

當你已進入那火焰
你開始視而不見
你會瘋狂去探索
從而找到滿足
在騷癢麻痺之中
我知道你享受其中
我的身體感到搖動
不需要害怕　　手繼續動
傷害不到因為珍重

繼續吧　　喘氣稍速
舌吻不需顧忌來放縱
我現在愛你　　你也會給我驚喜
不是個遊戲　　要放開那避忌
喔喔喔喔
進入深坑欣悅狂喜
不懷疑

情慾　　情慾
不是想像而是真實
情慾　　情慾
掏空失落填滿幸福
情慾　　情慾
蒙眼探索觸感刺激
情慾
情慾

情慾　　情慾
有大柱遮蔽含蓄羞恥
情慾　　放縱
將你我融入了自然　　喔喔喔喔
抽搐身體靈魂出竅
汗水滴進無底深處
歡樂應該兩情相悅
不需假裝流露自然
你很需要我
去為你作療癒　　（為你解放寂寥）
閉上眼睛

情慾　　情慾
情慾　　情慾　　（注入養料）
情慾　　情慾
情慾

情慾　　情慾
你令我迷失了那理智
因你身體
已佔據我

情慾　　（望著我　　你心動）
浪漫
連成一線邁向明天

情慾　（感覺到　　你深處）
激情
不知不覺已動聲色　　啊啊啊啊

情慾　（精壯的　　那身軀）
舒適
各有寶貝交換姓名

情慾
赤裸
將你身體跟我談情

不要停下那聲色
我們快樂無名
交換基因去刻劃本性
已銷魂到極

情慾

03.　情慾

Erotica
Romance
Erotica
Passion

I'm not your mistress   Nor am I your midnight cowboy
I'll be in charge of training tonight
Switch you from beginning to end
Put me into your head and then into your body
Will you be unable to extricate yourself
Let me be your lead and guide you the way you should go
No need to restrain yourself
Wander around with my hands and mouth

Stay or move forward
Enter the chest and then where to go
The feeling of love stays   Warming the entrance to the restricted area
You don't need to move   I'll press the switch
Your instinctive reaction   Is to expose everything nakedly   Oh Oh Oh Oh
I want to enter the end of your forest
And rivers

Erotica   Erotica
Find entrances from anywhere in your body
Erotica   Erotica
Find outlets everywhere in my body
Erotica
Stimulating

When you have entered the flame
You start to turn a blind eye
You will go crazy to explore
To find satisfaction
In the midst of itching numbness
I know you enjoy it
My body feels shaken
No need to be afraid   Just keep moving your hands
Can't be hurt because I cherish it

Go ahead   Breathe a little faster
French kiss is indulgent without any scruples
I love you now   You will surprise me too
It's not a game   You have to let go of your taboos   Oh Oh Oh Oh
Entering the pit of joy and ecstasy
No doubt

Erotica   Erotica
Not imagination but reality
Erotica   Erotica
Empty the loss and fill it with happiness
Erotica   Erotica
Explore tactile stimulation while blindfolded
Erotica
Erotica

Erotica   Erotica
There is a big pillar to hide the shame
Erotica   Indulgence
Integrate you and me into nature   Oh Oh Oh Oh
Twitching body and soul out of body
Sweat drips into the bottomless depths
Happiness should be mutual
No need to pretend to be natural
You need me very much
To heal you   (To liberate you from loneliness)
Close your eyes

Erotica   Erotica
Erotica   Erotica   (Inject nutrients)
Erotica   Erotica
Erotica

Erotica   Erotica
You made me lose my mind
Because of your body
Has taken possession of me

Erotica   (Looking at me   Have a crush on your heart)
Romance
Line up towards tomorrow

Erotica   (Feeling   Your deep inside)
Passion
Unknowingly I have been voiced out   Ah Ah Ah Ah

Erotica   (Muscular   That body)
Comfortable
Each has a baby and exchanges names

Erotica   Erotica
Naked
Use your body to talk about love with me

Don't stop that sound of lust
Our happiness is nameless
Swap genes to carve out your nature
Already in ecstasy

Erotica

03. Erotica

那一雙鞋不透明　　五光十色的外型
低筒長筒鞋履伴身影　　搭襯百變造型的襯衣
鑲著鑽石的玩意　　隨手塗鴉的創意
這是自我表現的日記
隨著心情

也許　　會認同這是年青
也許　　也感覺這是復興
哪怕是　　這是傭懶標誌
永遠堅持

一雙鞋代表愛情　　一雙鞋代表友情
難捨難分每段的距離
用這一雙鞋互相聯繫

一雙鞋代表安靜　　一雙鞋代表活力
動靜皆宜皆大都歡喜
各有道理

04.　一對 Converse 的思念

也許　　會穿著它遠足去
也許　　會穿著它去遊歷
沒限制　　年代裡每個衝擊
不會過期

對著一雙鞋回憶　　近的遠的不忘記
有笑有淚有痛有原因
是種紀錄生活的方式

那管你願不願意　　潮流未有分區別
一對 Converse　　是我的語言
La La La La....　　La La La La La La La
La La La La....

That pair of non-transparent shoes
Colourful appearance
High heel low heel shoes accompany my body and shadow
Lining to my everchanging clothes
The gadget of inlaying the diamonds
The creativity of ready graffiti
That is a diary of my performance
Depending on mood

Maybe   Will agree that is young
Maybe   Also feel that that is a revival
Even if   That is a sign of laziness
Persevere forever

A pair of shoes represents love
A pair of shoes represents friendship
It is difficult to leave and separate for each distance
Using a pair of shoes for a mutual connection

A pair of shoes represents calmness
A pair of shoes represents vitality
Everyone rejoices when both calmness and vitality are suitable
Each has its own sense

Maybe   Will put on it for hiking
Maybe   Will put on it for adventuring
No restriction   For every shock of eras
Will not expire

Memory arises when I look at the pair of shoes
Not forgetting those which were close or far
There must be reasons for having laughs tears and pains
It is a way of recording a living

No matter you are willing or not
No difference for trends
A pair of Converse   Is my language

La La La La.... La La La La La La La
La La La La....

04. Missing Of A Pair Of Converse

讓你的戰士打敗邪惡的一面，
解放你的光明。

Let your warrior defeat your
evil side and liberate your
brightness.

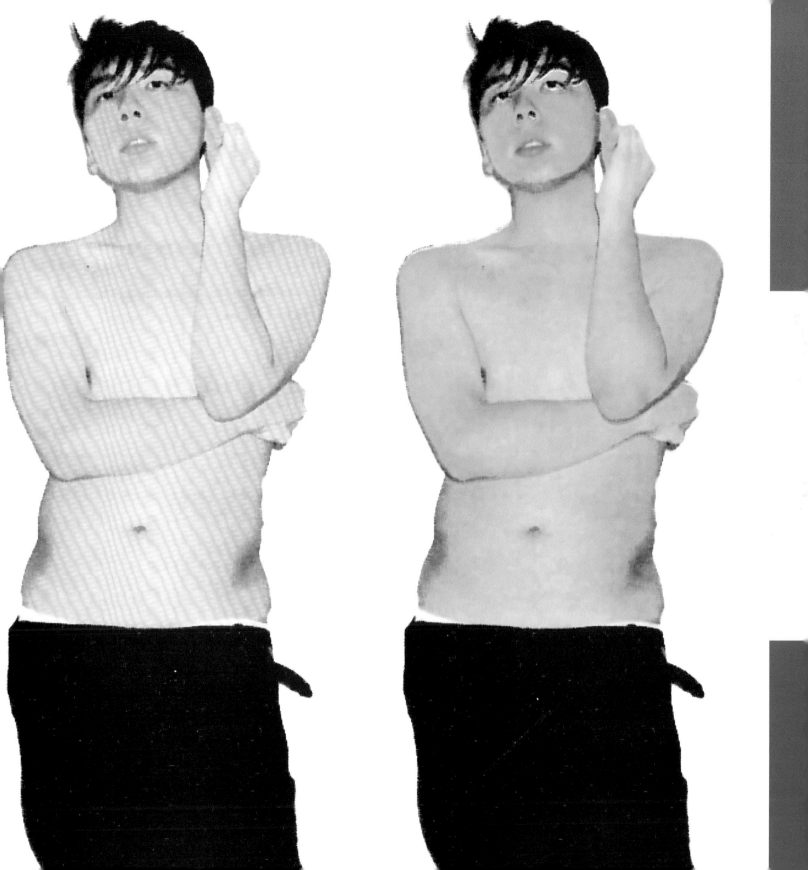

人生比你想像中脆弱　　平安需要遺囑給立下　　Ei Da Li Da La
不需要難過　　死後無牽掛　　Ei Da Li Da La
要笑著去揣摩　　杜絕眾相之爭
意外每天多　　自主恩賜誰　　太妙　太妙
看淡又怎麼　　沒人有權遞奪　　做人負責到底
不肯去面對　　放低心執著　　保險　意外　往生
這悲哀結果　　錢是身外物　　三寶　威力

不欲停留說話　　意外估計不了在何時
等身體僵硬化　　腦退化侵入
抬頭看不見　　昏迷還有意識
人家聽不到說話　　留彌的瞬間
心安理得接受　　需要人管理事
當肉身不在下　　授權書醫療指示
　　可免卻引起訴訟

Ei Da Li Da La
Ei Da Li Da La　　為何要想太多
　　一心一意去做　　**05.　平安（三寶）**

哭泣沒眼淚吧　　你沒有做錯
神經不動就塌　　不做就更加是錯
聽不到說話　　平安三寶做了
不知所措給嚇怕　　為自己人生辦妥
空間太革新吧
離開就放不下　　Ei Da Li Da La
　　Ei Da Li Da La
Ei Da Li Da La
Ei Da Li Da La　　找律師做三寶
　　無憂無慮生活
為何　為何　不平安　　不要計較金錢
後悔　後悔　後悔　　幾萬元不是什麼
做不了什麼　　如果不欲付出
　　意外往往會兌現

Life is more fragile than you think
No need to feel sad
To figure it out with a smile
Accidents happen every day
So what if one is bearish
Unwilling to face it
This sad result

Don't want to stop talking
Wait for the body to stiffen
Can't see when looking up
People can't hear what they say
Accept it with peace of mind
When the body is not around

Ei Da Li Da La
Ei Da Li Da La

Cry without tears
If the nerves don't move they will collapse
Can't hear speech
At a loss and scared
The space is too innovative isn't it
Can't let go if one leaves

Ei Da Li Da La
Ei Da Li Da La

Why   Why   Not peaceful
Regret   Regret   Regret   Nothing can be done

Peace requires a will
No worries after death
Put an end to conflicts among people
To whom is the gift of freedom given
No one has the right to take away
Let go of your attachments
Money is an external possession

Unable to estimate when accident will occur
Invalided by brain degeneration
Coma but still conscious
Be dying moment
Need people to manage things
Power of Attorney Advanced Directives
Can avoid litigation

Why think too much
Do it wholeheartedly
You do nothing wrong
Not doing it is even more wrong
The Three Instruments of Peace are made
Take care of your own life

Ei Da Li Da La
Ei Da Li Da La

Find a lawyer to do the Three Instruments of Peace
Carefree life
Don't worry about money
Tens of thousands of money is nothing
If you don't want to pay
Accidents often come true

Ei Da Li Da La
Ei Da Li Da La

So wonderful   So wonderful   Be responsible to the end
Insurance   Accident   Death
Three Instruments   Powerful

05. (Three Instruments) Of Peace

我不是你的奴隸或奴才之類
為什麼你要求盲目跟隨
大事春秋之際混扭成一堆
不會作任何犧牲
來成全你的私心去賣醉

狂風吹起謊言句
用我的愛受刑受罪
雷打喚醒人皆醉
付出真誠出賣碎

偽話儘量欺騙
夢話自說萬遍
痴話用來分隔我與你
各走各路璀璨完寂

一隻一隻螞蟻為后拋開了自尊
那其實縱容她致死
愚蠢的人群大多你我曾一起
不說現實唏噓
傷害過心會永牢記

沒有善男和信女
溫柔被霸道淹沒路退
迷痴被權力蒙閉
我不可被玩弄受罪

曾經甜言蜜語
曾經浪漫進睡
一切破滅忘了我是誰
幸好我勇敢去面對

判斷他說話
能夠相信嗎
無限地循環似是而非的道理
往六道說理
堅定用哲理
要分開彼此的原罪
各走各路不是逃避
各走各路遠離是非
給自己活好重生機

06. 各走各路

I'm not your slave or minion or anything like that
Why do you ask to follow blindly
During the significant events of Spring and Fall they get mixed up in a heap
Won't make any sacrifice
Come and fulfill your selfish desires and get drunk

The strong wind blows the lies
Being sinful and suffered from torture with my love
Thunder wakes the drunk ones
Give sincerity and sell everything into broken pieces

Lie as much as possible to deceive
Talk to yourself in thousands of times during your dreams
Silly words are used to separate you and me
Everyone goes their own way to end brightly

One by one the ants put aside their self-esteem for the queen
That would actually allow her to die
You and I were all long together in the stupid crowd
Don't talk about the reality as it's really sad
The heart that has been hurt will always be remembered

There are no good men or women
Gentleness is overwhelmed by domineering and retreats
Obsessed and blinded by power
I shall not be toyed with and suffered

Used to talk sweetly
Once fell asleep romantically
Everything is shattered and I forget who I am
Fortunately I have the courage to face it

Judge what he said
Can you believe it
Infinite looping the paradox of specious reason
Reasoning to the Six Paths
Use philosophy firmly
To separate each other's original sin
Going separate ways is not escaping
Go their separate ways and stay away from right and wrong
Live well and give yourself a new chance

06. Going Separate Ways

如果你不移走自己的內心的邪惡，就永遠不會做回自己和得到快樂。

If you don't remove your evil in your heart, you never be yourself and happy.

Ooh Ooh....　　Ooh La La
Ooh Ooh....　　Ooh La La

不會介意說我天真幼稚
思路清晰因為早立大志
珍藏珍惜幾十年的玩具
驚人意志和心力的年月

Ooh La La　　不會覺得喪智
Ooh La La　　喜歡不同玩兒
Ooh La La　　欣賞永不過時
Ooh La La　　紀錄每個心情

樂高積木山堆積
摩比大宅是甜蜜
Nanobloc 是世界的縮影
Megablock 有少見的主題

Ooh La La　　感謝各玩具
Ooh La La　　彌補我的空虛
Ooh La La　　陪我渡年月
Ooh La La　　重要的物品

Ooh Ooh....　　Ooh La La
Ooh Ooh....　　Ooh La La

做大收藏家　　從來沒有預算
樂意展示　　成立博物館園
讓大小一家　　討論歡迎拍照
安全樂園　　賞茶優閒聯誼

Oh La La　　不浪費時間
Oh La La　　金錢值得花掉
Oh La La　　反對看不起
Oh La La　　目光不要短視

你是我的忠實迷
支持博物館成立
我感謝你欣賞各玩具
快來看萬千品找回憶

Oh La La　　玩具不分齡
Oh La La　　也不區分膚色
Oh La La　　不屬於奢侈
Oh La La　　不代表幼稚

迪士尼收藏是大開眼界
蠟筆小新美少女戰士
叮噹芭比柯南小丸子
芝麻街 Muppets 還有孖寶兄弟

陳列在於此
紀錄在於此
(Ooh La La....　　Ooh La La)
歡樂在於此
(Ooh La La....
　Ooh Ooh....　　Ooh La La)

不是垃圾是寶物
每一件玩具均有價值
山珍海味食後終排泄
玩具經歷年代可流傳

Oh La La　　感謝我自己
Oh La La　　不理眼光冷視
Oh La la　　仍然繼續堅持
Oh la La　　收藏永無境止

Ooh La La....
Ooh La La....
Ooh La La

得著真有意思

Ooh La La....
Ooh La La....
Ooh La La

樂此不疲　　不分彼此

07.　玩具

Ooh Ooh....   Ooh La La
Ooh Ooh....   Ooh La La

Don't mind calling me naive
Thinking clearly because I set my ambition early
Toys cherished for decades
Years of amazing will and strength

Ooh La La   I won't feel stupid
Ooh La La   Likes to play different buddies
Ooh La La   Appreciation never gets old
Ooh La La   Record every mood

Lego bricks as mountain stack
Playmobil mansion is sweety
Nanoblock is a microcosm of the world
Megabloks has rare themes

Ooh La La   Thanks to all the toys
Ooh La La   Fill my void
Ooh La La   Accompany me through the years
Ooh La La   Important items

Ooh Ooh....   Ooh La La
Ooh Ooh....   Ooh La La

Become a big collector   Never have a budget
Happy to display   Establish a museum park
Let whole families   Discuss and take photos
Safe park   To enjoy tea and socialize

Oh La La   Don't waste time
Oh La La   Money is worth spending
Oh La La   Object and look down
Oh la la   Don't be short-sighted

You are my biggest fan
Support the establishment of the museum
I thank you for enjoying the toys
Come and see thousands of items to find memories

Oh La La   Toys for all ages
Oh La La   No distinction of races
Oh La La   Is not a luxurious
Oh La La   Doesn't mean childish

Disney collection is an eye-opening
Crayon Shin-chan Sailor Moon
Doraemon Barbie Detective Conan Chibi Maruko Chan
Sesame Street Muppets and Super Mario Bros

The display is here
The record is here   (Ooh La La.... Ooh La La)
Here lies the joy   (Ooh La La.... Ooh Ooh.... Ooh La La)

Not trash but treasure
Every toy has value
Excretion after eating delicacies from mountains and seas
Toys can be passed down timelessly

Oh La La   Thank myself
Oh La La   Ignore the cold gaze
Oh La la   Still keep on insisting
Oh la La   Collection never ends

Ooh La La....   Ooh La La....   Ooh La La
It's really interesting to get it
Ooh La La....   Ooh La La....   Ooh La La
Enjoy it endlessly
Without distinguishing between each other

07. Toys

煙花煙圈在空氣趕跑
趕在蒸發人間的瞬秒
尚在人間的味道
刺鼻也不好
他知道　　她都知道

不要情調
快戒掉　　心情反覆給鎖掉
不能怪罪予別人不好
太煩擾　　煩惱心情就不好
少了樂趣
空氣少了煙號
聞不到那浮躁

型不在於一支煙的依靠
灑脫不等於吸煙姿勢好
不要污染我面頰
雙唇也不好
我不屑　　快滾掉

快來戒掉
戒得掉　　在乎誰不心搖
身體警號無處可逃
不再逃　　或延期去明瞭
拿著煙不點火覺無聊

不可靠　　煙草味唱反調
不需清高和高尚情操
不愛他　　也不愛她瘋掉
像癮君子迷幻生活
空氣維持單調
身體維持良好

心理質素美好
關係回復可靠

08.　不愛吸煙的人

Fireworks' smoky rings chase away in the air
Evaporate in the blink of an eye in a second
The taste remains in the world
Pungent is not good either
He knows   And she knows

Don't be sentimental
Quit quickly   My mood is locked again and again
Cannot blame others for your badness
Too much trouble   Worry makes you feel bad
Less fun
The air is less smokey
Can't smell that fickleness

Coolness does not depend on a cigarette
Being free and easy does not mean having a good smoking posture
Don't pollute my cheeks
My lips are not good either
I don't care   Get out of here

Come and quit
If you can quit   It doesn't matter who you are
There is no escape from warning sign of a body
No more escaping   Or postponing to find out
Feeling bored holding a cigarette without lighting it

Unreliable   Tobacco smells act in contrary
No need for loftiness and noble sentiments
I don't love him   And I don't love her crazy either
Like an addict's psychedelic life
The air remains monotonous
Maintain good health
Good psychological quality
Restore the reliable relationship

08. Don't Like Those Who Smoke Cigarettes

儒夫將放棄自己的烈火，
而戰士將擊敗一切阻礙他／她
的東西。

A coward will give up his/her
burning fire whereas a fighter
will defeat everything which
blocks him/her.

哪裡有幸運的星
不再為那無聊愛花心思
擁抱的甜蜜
不給予否定
太多的雜念
讓我不專心

光芒　　光芒
我積極去尋覓
光芒　　光芒
不用替我著急
光芒　　光芒
祈求幸運到底
光芒　　光芒　　Yeah

你是否那幸運星
默默在背後付出與支持
當我迷失時
有你在照明
有你在背後
我更加堅定

光明　　光明
一路有守護靈
光明　　光明
不許黑暗榮耀
光明　　光明
樂於引導致勝
光明　　光明　　Yeah

過來　　讓負能量擺脫要鎮定
放負不是一個方法讓自己獲益
喔　　過來　　客套說法不是一回事
因為凡事有因必有果就是

幸運星或許是你
不用猜度或懷疑
每個人有幸運星
在身旁不可否認

光星　　光星
我在閃亮不停
光星　　光星
不分晝夜進行
光星　　光星
實體不是透明
光星　　光星　　Yeah

幸運星到處皆是
茫茫人海會浮現
幸運星不需證明
自然感覺在心裡
幸運星永恆或許
緣起緣滅也或許
（將幸運降臨　　Baby）
幸運星沒有分明
成另一個幸運星

星塵　　星塵
宇宙浩瀚著迷
星塵　　星塵
我欲去你帶領
星塵　　星塵
我幸運還有你

光芒　　光芒
你將厄運揮灑去
真的感謝你　　Baby
無時無刻都伴我同行
光明　　光明
光星　　光星
星塵　　星塵
光影　　光影
光景　　光景　　Baby
幸運　　幸運
有你時刻扶持
沒有你怎辦　　Baby
失去你　　失散了怎辦　　Baby
你要永遠給我支持
你是我的幸運星

09. Lucky Star

Where is the lucky star
Stop worrying about boring love
The sweetness of hugs
Don´t deny
Too many distracting thoughts
Let me not concentrate

Radiance   Radiance
I actively search for
Radiance   Radiance
Don´t worry about me
Radiance   Radiance
Praying for luck to the end
Radiance   Radiance   Yeah

Are you that lucky star
Silently giving and supporting behind the scenes
When I am lost
You are lighting up
With you behind my back
I am more determined

Brightness   Brightness
There is a guardian spirit along the way
Brightness   Brightness
No dark glory allowed
Brightness   Brightness
Willing to lead to victory
Brightness   Brightness   Yeah

Come here
Let go of the negative energy and stay calm
Letting go of burdens is not a way to benefit yourself
Oh   Come here   It´s nothing to say nice things
Because everything has a cause and must have a result

The lucky star may be you
No need to guess or doubt
Everyone has a lucky star
It is undeniable that it is by their side

Radiance   Radiance

I´m shining
Radiance   Radiance
Carry out day and night
Radiance   Radiance
Entity is not transparent
Radiance   Radiance   Yeah

Lucky stars are everywhere
And appear in the vast sea of people
Lucky stars don´t need to be proven
They naturally feel in the heart
Maybe the lucky star will be eternal
Or maybe it will be appear and leave with the fate
(Bring luck to ones   Baby)
The lucky star is not clear
It becomes another lucky star

Stardust   Stardust
Fascinated by the vastness of the universe
stardust   Stardust
I want to go and you lead me
stardust   Stardust
I´m lucky to still have you
Stardust   Stardust

Radiance   Radiance
You throw away my bad luck
Thank you so much   Baby
Accompany me all the time
Brightness   Brightness
Light star   Light star
Stardust   Stardust
Light and shadow   Light and shadow
Spectacle   Spectacle   Baby
Lucky   Lucky
You always support me
What would I do without you   Baby
Losing you   What should I do   Baby
You must always support me
You are my lucky star

09. Lucky Star

Er Er Er Er Er Ey-yeah　　Er Er Er Er Er Ey-yeah
Er Er Er Er Er Ey-yeah　　Er Er Er Er Er Ey-yeah
Er Er Er Er Er Ey-yeah　　Er Er Er Er Er Ey-yeah
Er Er Er Er Er Ey-yeah　　Er Er Er Er Er Ey-yeah

美麗的掙扎在於年紀上升的危機
皺紋在臉眼頸上表露了歲月疤痕
體力下降不再輕易跳轉失了平衡
糖尿病肥胖缺血性中風心臟衰竭
像過山車般心情上落差大傷了神
狀態不勇回復不了年輕快樂光陰
再不能賣弄姿色盡情享樂和銷魂
不欲看見身型鬆弛成了個人敗筆

你準備　　準備　　準備去服用
你不會　　不會　　不會有顧忌

NMN　　需要你予我補給
NMN　　每天只需吃一粒　　Yeah
NMN　　我要　　NMN
不要跟年紀上升衰老做不到找不到年輕
NMN　　沒有它活不了命
就是　　NMN　　賦予我第二生命
NMN　　我要　　NMN

想回復肌膚彈性柔軟光滑再重生
想新陳代謝速度像年輕維持平均
維持血管健康和減低病患的風險
延遲衰老強化肌肉抗氧化可平衡

能量轉換加快使身體發炎不長行
預防動脈粥樣硬化和改善心血管
改善器官的勞損防止急病的發生
N-N-N-M-M-M-M-N-N-N-N-N-M-N
N-N-N-M-M-M-M-N-N-N-N-N-M-N

你全心全意　　相信　　相信它的功用

NMN　　睡覺我不再扎醒
NMN　　精神充足賞風景
NMN　　每天的補充　　Yeah
不再陷入困擾擔心年老被年輕人打敗本性
NMN　　魅力增加顯信心
NMN　　身心健康活動年輕
NMN　　就是 NMN
修復身體內外一切歲月殘酷留下的痕跡

NMN　　縱然有療效功用
NMN　　目前還沒判斷副作用
NMN　　上癮還沒證實
每天可以服用一定毫克分量助提升

Oh Ey-yeah Oh Oh　　Oh Oh Ey-yeah
Oh Ey-yeah Oh Oh　　Oh Oh Ey-yeah
Oh Ey-yeah Oh Oh　　Oh Oh Ey-yeah
Oh Ey-yeah Oh Oh　　Oh Oh Ey-yeah

Oh Ey-yeah Oh Oh　　Oh Oh Ey-yeah
Oh Ey-yeah Oh Oh　　Oh Oh Ey-yeah
Oh Ey-yeah Oh Oh　　Oh Oh Ey-yeah

10.　NMN

Er Er Er Er Er Ey-yeah   Er Er Er Er Er Ey-yeah
Er Er Er Er Er Ey-yeah   Er Er Er Er Er Ey-yeah
Er Er Er Er Er Ey-yeah   Er Er Er Er Er Ey-yeah
Er Er Er Er Er Ey-yeah   Er Er Er Er Er Ey-yeah

The beautiful struggle lies in the crisis of aging
Wrinkles on the face eyes and neck reveal the scars of time
When physical strength decreases
-it is no longer easy to jump turn around and lose balance
Diabetes Obesity Ischemic stroke Heart failure
It's like a roller coaster and the emotional gap is very frustrating
The bad condition cannot be able to restore one's youthful and happy days
No longer show off one's beauty and have fun and ecstasy
Don't want to see a flabby body shape and become a personal failure

Are you ready   Ready   Ready to take it
You won't   Won't   Won't have scruples

NMN   Needs it to give me supplies
NMN   Just take one pill a day   Yeah
NMN   I want NMN
Don't get older and decrepit which one can't find youth anymore
NMN   Can't live without it
That is MNM   Give one a second life
NMN   I want NMN

Want to restore skin elasticity softness smoothness and rebirth
Want to maintain an average metabolic rate like a young person
Maintain blood vessel health and reduce patient risk
Delay aging strengthen muscles antioxidant and to strike for balance
Accelerated energy conversion makes the body inflamed and indigestible
Prevent atherosclerosis and improve cardiovascular disease
Improve organ strain and prevent acute illness
N-N-N-M-M-M-M-M-N-N-N-N-N-M-N
N-N-N-M-M-M-M-M-N-N-N-N-N-M-N

You believe it with all your heart   Believe   Believe it works

NMN   I won't wake up when I sleep
NMN   Is energetic enough to enjoy the scenery
NMN   Daily supplement   Yeah
No longer trapped in worries about old age and being defeated by young people
NMN   Charm increases confidence
NMN   Physical and mental health activities to stay young
NMN   That is NMN
Repair all the traces left by the cruelty of time inside and outside the body

NMN   Even has therapeutic effects
NMN   Has not determined the side effects yet
NMN   Addiction has not been proven
Can take certain mg per day to help promotion

Oh Ey-yeah Oh Oh   Oh Oh Ey-yeah
Oh Ey-yeah Oh Oh   Oh Oh Ey-yeah
Oh Ey-yeah Oh Oh   Oh Oh Ey-yeah
Oh Ey-yeah Oh Oh   Oh Oh Ey-yeah

Oh Ey-yeah Oh Oh   Oh Oh Ey-yeah
Oh Ey-yeah Oh Oh   Oh Oh Ey-yeah
Oh Ey-yeah Oh Oh   Oh Oh Ey-yeah

10. NMN

成為身體的國王，成為臉龐的
女皇。

Be a king of your body and be a
queen of your face.

夜鏡透視　　無人四野
黑暗進行　　措手不及
迷彩軍衣　　埋伏不見
一聲指令　　攻擊乍現

戰俘在撕吼虐刑不能看到天日會出現
警號響起年和月

無情的戰火　　四周在蔓延
無止境燃燒文明作業
子彈在橫飛　　不需問
為何人只為貪念奉獻

戰役在世界重現
道德沒有那底線
生命每天被威脅
廢墟中渡過每夜

搶劫浩蕩　　暴動頻見
沒有理性　　沒有愛念
灰色黑空　　毒氣四溢
不能逃避　　無奈迎拴接

慰安婦遭凌遲悲慘到伸手而不見
擔驚受怕遭消滅

日夜的槍戰　　坦克車過千
軍機在天空周旋殺獵
原子彈出現　　轟炸了城邊
一秒給溶化四肢分裂

生命塗炭霜加雪
血染成河太慘烈
屍體殘肢在遍野
惡夢重覆會瘋癲

你有聽見我　　（聽見）
你在聽見我　　（聽見）

血腥在囚室裡面慘叫不禁看見　　（恐見）
哪有人同情那些無辜死難弱者　　（慘烈）

核爆力無限　　震動了地殼
連帶著天災摧毀世界
人不能幸免　　難逃這浩劫
生存並沒有希望活著

暴烈戰鬥不夜天
繁華社會不復見
麻木對待這世界
永不止息的戰爭

11. 戰爭

Looking through the night vision google   No one is in the wild
Get on in the dark   Catch off guard
Camouflage military uniform   Ambush unseen
One command   Attack appears

The war's prisoners are growling and tortured
-which can't look at the appearance of a day and the sky
The siren is alarmed in years and months

Relentless war and fire   Spreading all around
Burning all civilized works endlessly
The bullets are flying   No need to ask the God
Why humans are only for greedy mind and dedication

The battles reappear in the world
Morality has no that bottom line
Life is threatened every day
Spending every night in the ruins

Robbery is widespread   Riots are frequently seen
Can't escape
No rationality   No mind of love
Grey and dark sky   Poisonous gas is in everywhere
Can't escape   Sad to accept

It is tragic that comfort women are suffered from
-harassment and punishment without seeing they reach out their hands
Fear of being destroyed

Gun battles in days and nights   Over thousands of tanks
Military aircraft are hunting in the sky
Atomic bombs appear   Bombing at the side of cities
Four limbs are split and melted in one second

Life be ashes and make things worse
Rivers are dyed with blood which is too tragic
Corpses and split limbs are in everywhere
Repeated nightmares can make you crazy

Have you listened to what I say   (Listen)
Have you listened to what I say   (Listen)

Bloody violence and screams inside
-the cell which can't stop seeing   (Fear to see)
Who sympathizes with the innocent dead and the weak persons   (Tragic)

The nuclear explosion is infinitely   Shaking the crust
Destroy the world with natural disasters
The human cannot be fortunately avoided
To escape that catastrophe
There is no hope of survival

Fierce battles are never ended
No longer seeing prosperous society
Numbness to treat that world
Never ending wars

11. Wars

今天覺得很憂鬱　　都是因為著你
你的魅力我肯定　　在我心不停止
得到你給我的愛　　得到你將事排外
留給你我的全部真誠相待
忘不了你留給我情載

朋友們喚勸我　　找一個男去愛
我沒有兩小無猜　　學習怎樣看待
愛情盲目猜不來　　自由選擇看未來
到目前為止　　只有你可依賴
吻著我的傷口藉慰耐

你給我承諾　　發展地下情等待
浮不出面　　有時難耐
但期待一晚赤裸跟我纏綿放開
這到底是幻想或實在

你有你的家庭　　我還是一人呆
聽你聲音磁帶　　滿足我心安懷
一次給你競賽　　一次給我轉載
不論在不在　　我都釋懷
你愛我　　偷偷激烈去愛

沒另個女人　　讓你割捨離開
那片段　　在腦海　　感覺鬚根觸動心海
吻著雙唇蠕動身體樂得自在

重回你正軌生活
我接受關係已告落
再見　　找另個像你
愛我
親我
哄我

你愛我
偷偷激烈去愛
浮不出面
有時難耐

沒另個女人
讓你割捨離開
重回你正軌生活

12.　情婦的告白

feel so sad and depress today   Because of you
assure your charm   Is in my heart without stopping
To get the love you give me   Excluding all matters outside for having you
Leaving you with all my sincerity
I can't forget the love experience you gave me

Friends ask me   To find a man to love
I don't have puppy lovers   To learn how to treat each other
Love can't guess blindly   See the future with free choice
Up till now   Only you can be relied on
Kissing my wound to comfort my loneliness

You give me a promise   To wait and develop a secret love affair
Can't show up   Sometimes unbearable
But looking forward to be naked with me and linger for a night
Is this a fantasy or a reality

You have your family   I still stay alone
Listen to your voice tape   To satisfy my heart
Once for you to contest   Once for me to reprint
No matter if I am here or not   I will be relieved
You love me   Secretly and intensely to love

There is no other woman   To let you give up and leave
That scene   Is in my head   Feeling the stubble touching my sea of heart
Kissing your lips and wriggling our bodies happily and freely

Return to your right track of life
I accept the relationship has ended
Goodbye   Find another like you
Love me
Kiss Me
Coax me

You love me   Secretly and intensely to love
Can't show up   Sometimes unbearable

There is no other woman   To let you give up and leave
Return to your right track of life

12. Confession Of A Mistress

沒有劇本的戲劇一向具有戲劇
性和令人難以置信。

No script for a play is always
dramatic and incredible.

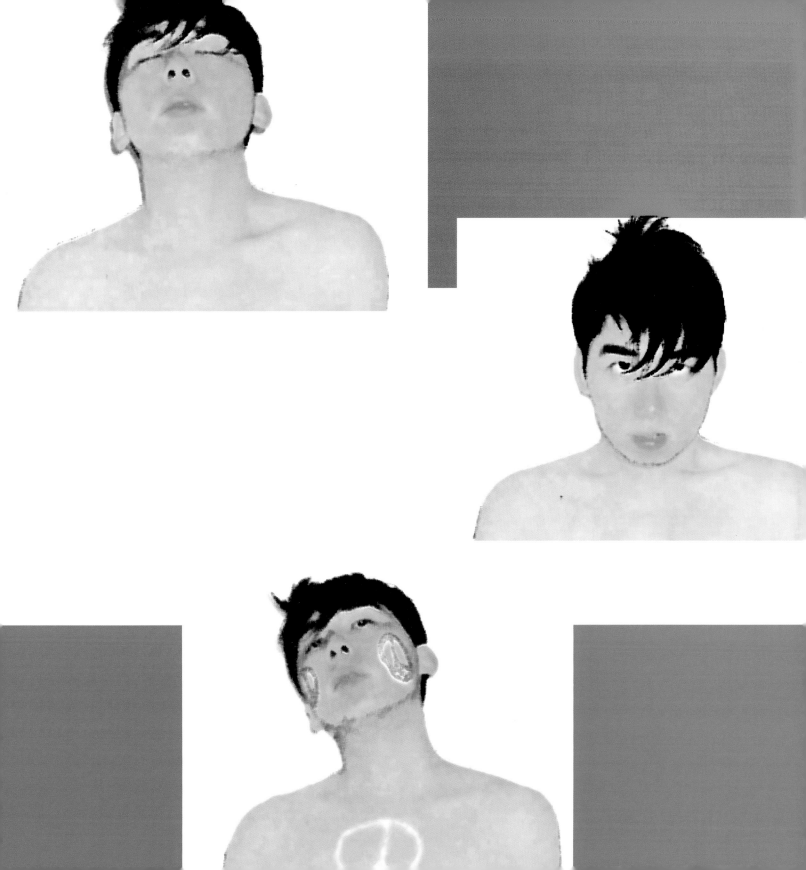

天陰暗　　風起了
Rain　　雨終到來纏繞著
我思念掛在天空心平靜不來
Rain　　洗去我的擔憂
對未知未來該走向哪方平安
Rain

生存為了找什麼
愛與被愛的換來是失落
我哼著那一首歌
你有否聽著
我知道這場雨想告訴我不需想多
命皆尤地就該隨意去過
執著行事總會引起禍
在高峰看雨水瘋狂嘀嗒掉落

歡樂迎接
Rain　　讓世間戾氣洗掉
人間有恨也有愛
不該愛都錯愛過
不該恨都錯恨不能回頭逆轉
Rain　　愛不需要去襯托
不需要向別人同情交代分享
Rain

雨灑落赤裸身軀
肉帛而相見　　你看到什麼
傷痕累累的疤痕
還能說什麼
親吻我撫慰我空虛內心的不安

雨看見我們共同失望
洗滌我們負能量散掉
現在等陰天快過　　太陽送溫暖

不能擺脫
Rain　　讓不快盡快消失
讓不安一同去洗掉重新感覺
Rain　　將悲傷去抹掉
歸過一個真正的我完整的我

雨過天晴
陽光溫暖
告訴我　　浴火後重生

等待是漫長的事　　（總是）
（天意弄人總是如此）　　想要的東西偏偏給不了
唯有進夢　　（痴人說夢總會醒）
情緒起伏總免不了　　（易怒易動武）
自由不是無限　　（道德論說）
（神奇的是這天地）　　無時無刻變天氣
（雨狂下）　　意料之內下　　不出奇
（雨停了）　　不是作告別　　休息

雨是風暴給予成
我的心靈　　聽見大自然聲
自求多福　　災害不會少
後知後覺人總沒有意識危險
什麼感覺
Rain

感覺到　　就來臨
暴風雨欲前來
Rain
想不到　　就來臨
雨水能可打救

Rain　　洗滌大地的污穢
洗滌大地人的沈倫逆天墮落
Rain　　重整大地生活
解開被人鎖上一群無辜心靈
Rain

就是雨　　沖洗了
這污穢大地
Rain
重生了　　新生活
不需去解說

正面正義正道的人
值得留下在這大地
Rain

13. Rain

The sky is dark and the wind is blowing
Rain   The rain will eventually come and surround ones
My thoughts are hanging in the sky and my heart can't calm down
Rain   Washes away my worries
Be safe in the unknown direction of the future
Rain

What are you looking for to survive
Loving and being loved results in loss
  hum that song
Are you listening
  know this rain wants to tell me that I don't need to think too much
If you are destined to be in a special place you should go there freely
Acting persistently will always lead to disaster
Watching the rain falling crazily at the peak

Happy greeting
Rain   Washes away the rage in the world
There is hate and there is love in the world
  shouldn't have loved but I loved it by mistake
  shouldn't hate it as it's all wrong which I turn around and reverse it
Rain   Love doesn't need to be foiled
No need to express sympathy and share with others
Rain

Rain falls on naked body
When we meet each other nakedly   What do you see
Scarred scars
What else can be said
Kiss me and soothe the restlessness in my empty heart
The rain sees us disappointed together
Wash away our negative energy
Now wait for the cloudy days to pass   And the sun to bring warmth

Can't get rid of
Rain   Makes the unpleasantness disappear as soon as possible
Let the uneasiness wash away and have new feeling again
Rain   Erases sadness
Return to a real me and complete me

Sunny after rain
The sun is warm
Tell me   Re-born from the ashes

Waiting is a long time   (Always)
(This is always the case with God's will)   I can't give you what I want
Only dreaming   (Idiots say dreams will always wake up)
Emotional ups and downs are inevitable   (Irritable and prone to violence)
Freedom is not unlimited   (Moral theory)
(The magic is this world)   The weather changes all the time
(Rain falls wildly)   It's expected and not surprising
(The rain stopped)   Not saying goodbye   Resting

Rain is given by the storm
My soul   Hears the sound of nature
Ask for more blessings   There will be no less disasters
People who realize in hindsight never realize the danger
What does it feel like
Rain

When you feel it   It's coming
The storm is coming
Rain
Coming   Unexpectedly
Rain can save you

Rain   Washes away the dirt of the earth
Cleansed the earth and people who are degrading and fallen against the will of heaven
Rain   Restores life on earth
Unlock a group of innocent hearts locked up by others
Rain

It's the rain   Washed it away
This filthy earth
Rain
Reborn   New life
No need to explain

Positive and righteous person
Worth staying in this land
Rain

13. Rain

人如常在工作
社會如常運作
仿如天下太平
常規下去生活
多勞多得是對
學習是無止境
為糊口而對出
放棄清晰追索

到底是為誰而去工作
社會是如此的正確
一群人卻在黑暗活動
Ooh Ooh Ooh
人不加以思索
Ooh Ooh Ooh
是愚蠢或懶惰
Ooh Ooh Ooh
是放縱或冷漠
造就犯罪黑幕

大群人勤勞工作
比不上奢華生活
行頭名牌傾出多
以為身份不拆破
上億身家再貪多
不理最後玩出禍
賭博心態不覺錯
用全錢叫鬼推磨

把黑錢散落在正道
飲食娛樂地產財務
打本給下屬共同流
Ooh Ooh Ooh

那娛樂的大亨
Ooh Ooh Ooh
這地產的大亨
Ooh Ooh Ooh
那金融的大鱷
這商業的奇才

由陰謀去主宰
Oh Oh Oh Oh Oh Oh

世界每個角落　　（角落）
貧富極度懸殊　　（懸殊）
精英善用物質
宣傳到很神聖投地
馴服人拋棄和平自然

洗黑錢能致富
（犯法又如何）
洗黑錢是機遇
（錯誤的觀念）
洗黑錢很誘惑
（命危在旦夕）
洗黑錢有權力
（沒有好下場）

嘲笑常人太苯
（金融完結錢空沒了）
虛偽大慈善家
（財庫一下變窮可笑）
沒理會那下場
（將靈魂奉獻給魔鬼）
自作孽不可活

14.　AML

People are working as usual
Society is operated as usual
As if the world is at peace
Living under norms
It's right that hard work pays more
Learning is endless
To meet the ends for living
Renouncing clear recourse

Who are you working for
Society is so right
A group of people are working in the dark
Ooh Ooh Ooh
People without thinking
Ooh Ooh Ooh
Is stupid or lazy
Ooh Ooh Ooh
Indulgence or indifference
Bring up crime shady

Large group of people working hard
Not as good as having luxury life
There are many famous brands in the outfit
Don't think his identity will be exposed
Keeping on greedy with a net worth of hundreds of millions
Ignore the calamity of the game in the end
Don't feel wrong for gambling mentality
Using money to tell ghosts to turn the mill

Scatter the black money in the right way
Catering Entertainment Real Estate Finance
Paying capitals for subordinates for collusion
Ooh Ooh Ooh

That entertainment tycoon
Ooh Ooh Ooh
This real estate tycoon
Ooh Ooh Ooh
That financial predators
This business genius

Ruled by conspiracy
Oh Oh Oh Oh Oh Oh Oh Oh

Every corner of the world   (Corner)
Great disparity between rich and poor   (Disparity)
The elites make good use of material
Propaganda is very sacred and pleased
Taming mankind to abandon peaceful nature

Money laundering can get one rich
(So what about breaking the law)
Money laundering is an opportunity
(Wrong concept)
Money laundering is tempting
(Life is at stake)
Money laundering has power
(No good end)

Laughing at the stupid ordinary people
(Finance is over and no more wealth and money)
Hypocritical philanthropist
(It's ridiculous that the treasury suddenly becomes poor)
Ignoring that fate
(Dedicate his soul to the devil)
Self-making sin makes one no longer live

14. AML

赤身裸體，你會知道你失去了
什麼。

Be naked and you will know
what you have lost.

原野下溫暖陽光
映照小麥長大
動人的童話不朽傳
找方向

世界大人太複雜
社會演變真快
感動是否觸情感
裝模樣

小孩　　往哪兒漂泊他方
捉迷藏　　活潑玩耍
真太平安
灌輸愛的代價

Mm. . . .　Or　Mm. . . .

幸福不是必然的
有些小孩相反
在戰壕中擔驚受怕
明天或許往天堂

小孩是活力之泉
但不可溺愛他
告訴他現實與幻想　　大落差

小孩　　情緒可毀了大志
抱著我　　安穩心情
淡定冷靜
不比較和競爭

小孩要勇敢
小孩學懂嗎
長大後世界怎樣
做好自己就足夠
真的　　小孩

15. 孩子

Warm sunshine in the wilderness
Growing up in the light of wheat
The touching immortal fairy tale
Finding direction

The world is too complicated
Society evolves so fast
Is touching arousing emotions
Pretending

Child   Where are you wandering
Hide and seek   Playing lively
So peaceful
Instilling the cost of love
Mm.... Or Mm....

Happiness is not inevitable
Some children are in the opposite
Terrifying in the trenches at war
Maybe go to heaven tomorrow

Child is the source of vitality
But don't spoil him
Tell him between reality and fantasy   The gap is big

Child   Emotion can ruin ambition
Hold me   Calm my mind
Keep calm and calm down
Don't compare and compete

Child must be brave
Does child understand
What will the world be like when you grow up
It's enough to be yourself
It's real   Child

15. Child

男女情愛之間
離不開親蜜中愛慾的感覺
造愛享受纏綿
佔據身體每一部份到永遠
畫面不變　　不需語言
沈默地激情吻遍心想保存
政客遠見　　不理入眠
等待晚上溫暖擁著纏綿

喘氣聲是音樂
不能排練是真實一刻傳染
赤裸肉帛相見
不會尷尬忘記了性別歧視
晴天雨天　　沒有分別
是兩個人花房遊戲人間
新聞報導　　視而不見
有什麼重要過關係透解

繼續吧
推前擁後無法控制了知覺
享受吧
聞到雙方的體味渾發在空氣裡面
原始吧
實在吧
不要誰給答案　　不要誰負責問號
放心吧
就這一刻　　　解放全面

人類選擇　　最後感傷
最後感傷
最後感傷

不需要著承諾
如果計較太重於情感之間
不至於情愛的
人類互相適應衝動要纏綿
太久膩了　　換個新鮮
都市裡人群追求刺激的無邊
亂了每夜　　只求一夜
但願浪漫激情溶他乾烈
享受吧

一刻溫馨一刻動容的心情
難說吧
徹底吧
相信一切真實情人的剖白
難忘吧

醒來吧
情人在那床單
情人或許離開了
心傷吧

16. 造愛後人類感傷

The love between boy and girl
In-separate the feeling of love and sex of intimacy
Enjoy lingering during lovemaking
Occupy every part of the body
The screen is unchanged   No language
Passionate kisses secretly which the hearts want to preserve
Politician foresight   Don't care and sleep
Waiting for having a warm hug and lingered at night

Wheeze is music
Cannot rehearse and is real for a moment of infection
Seeing each other naked
No embarrassment and forgetting sexual discrimination
Shiny day rainy day   No difference
Is the human game inside the garden room for two persons
News report   Seeing but not have seen
What is more important than of the transparent interpretation of a relationship

Continue
Push forward and backwards which can't control the perception
Enjoy it
Smell the body odour of each other which it volatilizes in the air
Original
Realistic
Don' give anybody answer   Don't ask anybody bear the question mark
Don't worry
At this moment   Full liberation
No need to promise
If you care too much about feelings
That's not love
Humans adapt to each other and should impulse and linger
I'm tired of too long   Change a fresh one
The endless pursuit of excitement by the crowd in the city
Chaos every night   Just for one night
I hope romance and passion would melt him
Enjoy it

A moment of warmness a moment of dynamic mood
Hard to say it
Thoroughly
Believe every real explanation of the lover
Unforgettable

Wake up
The lover is on that bedsheet
Lover perhaps has been left
Heartbroken

The choice of human   Last sadness
Last sadness
Last sadness

16. Humans Are Sad After Lovemaking

赤身裸體，你會知道哪個身體部位最美麗。

Be naked and you will know which bodily part is the most beautiful.

畢竟人是自私　　自大的
永遠不想吃酸中帶香的蘋果
人總不能像花能夠自然結果
人像萬花筒　　千變萬化
圖案雖美　　但這都是被塑造出來
人生如夢　　永遠到死後
才能知曉真正結果

萬花筒的圖案千變萬化
每個角度看都不同
要真正了解其圖案的構造
都好像是一場夢
人生不需要固執地追究其變化的處境
只要明白無常之美
便能明白人生到底是怎樣的一回事

17.　萬花筒

After all humans are selfish and arrogant
Never want to eat a smelly but sour apples
Humans always cannot like flowers which bear fruit
Humans like kaleidoscopes   Everchanging
Although the patterns are beautiful   These are being shaped
Life likes dream   Till to death forever
Then can know the true result

Although the patterns of kaleidoscopes are everchanging
They are different to look at a particular angle
To really know more about the structure of such patterns
It likes a dream
Life needs not stubbornly to pursue such a changing situation
Only need to understand the beauty of Impermanence
Then you can understand what life is about

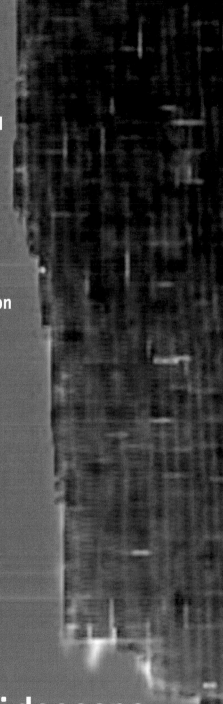

17. Kaleidoscope

太久了　承受那不該承受了
無聲　那代表了什麼心聲
習慣　無伴在左右渡過了時光
無熱鬧情景空洞了
看日落　泛黃色隨心所欲飄泊
觸情　手不放下十指緊扣
回憶　是最殘酷但最美的珍藏
是誰叫喚誰的思盼

放下你　所愛的那人
讓他追逐自己旅程
兩個人　風雨經歷過
該成熟認真
放下你　所愛的那人
該明白塵俗的緣份
屬於誰太執著讓人
下沉

沒有他　生活該展開另一頁了
情感　不多不少會不安穩
忘記　心太多故慮為何要去等
若愛他　該祝福不等

無法預測　未來兩人
各有所屬　點滴人生
展開旅程　新的沖擊
過得更豐盛

放下你　所愛的那人
若愛他　不要再下沉
祝福他　尋找另一個
愛著他的人
放下你　所愛的那人
接受那一刻的單程
成回憶　更好的在前
默等

18. 放下你　所愛的人

It's been a long time   It shouldn't be bearable
Silent   What does that represent
I'm used to   Spending time without a partner
No lively scene is empty
Watching the sunset   It turns yellow and drifts as you like
Touching   Hands don't let go
Memories   Are the cruelest but most beautiful treasures
Who is calling who's looking to

Let go   Of the one you love
Let him chase his own journey
Two people   Have experienced the storm
Should be mature seriously
Let go   Of the one you love
Should understand the fate of the mundane
Belong to who is too persistent
Sinking

Without him   Life would have opened another page
Emotions   Will not be more or less stable
Forget   I have too much heart so why should I wait
If you love him   You should be blessed

Unpredictable   Two people in the future
Each has its own   Bit of life
Start a journey   New shock
Live more abundantly

Let go   Of the one you love
If you love him   Don't sink anymore
Bless him   And find another
Love those who love him
Let go   Of the one you love
Accept a one-way ride at that moment
Become a memory   Better ahead
Wait silently

18. Let Go Of The One You Love

怪胎可能並不惹人討厭，但混
蛋一定會。

A freak may not be nasty but a
jerk must definitely be.

程式　智能　編碼　設計
四肢與思想連繫
能言善辯溝通
在這地

觀察　人類表情
訊息　傳染
別有用心地栽培
是否另有目的

科技太過先進與物質
不許退步也不算是有共鳴
信依賴人工智能
方便生活旋律
連它都能操控天氣

策劃　一場動義
反轉　天地
人類是那麼迷信
反被人類禍起

大眾往往是被動覺得乏味
貪圖安逸讓腦退化永理虧
沒有思想去判斷
根據生活所需
危機處理喪失敗了天敵

機器人侵入了人類自生權利
代替了勞動或精英的原位
甘心被丟入廢墟
反自然的本質
違背天意淘汰自己

淘汰（人類）　淘汰（人類）

等一天殲滅人類
萬劫不復　太遲
我們要覺醒　不後悔

19.　AI

Program Smart Coding Design
Connecting limbs and mind
Eloquent communication
It's here

Observe Human expressions
Message Infection
Cultivate with ulterior motives
Is there another purpose

Technology is too advanced and material
Not being allowed to step back is not considered a resonance
Faith relies on artificial intelligence
Convenient life's melody
Even it can control the weather

Plan An insurrection
Reverse The World
Humans are so superstitious
But is caused by the mankind

The public is often passive and finds it boring
Coveting comfort makes the brain degenerate forever
No thought to judge
According to the needs of life
Crisis management lost the natural enemy

Robots invade human survival rights
In place of labor or elite
Willing to be thrown into ruins
Anti-natural essence
Eliminate oneself against the God's will

Knock Out (Humans) Knock Out (Humans)

Wait for a day to wipe out human beings
Beyond redemption It's too late
We have to wake up Without regret

19. AI

三分鐘的聆訊進行
你爭我議通訊中
延長期限遞交文件
或申請修改申述
或加入刪減訟方
或終止代表客人
這簡單要求　申請　不需　出庭抗辯

為何雙方見面
向官去解釋
像後宮存之道
往往爾虞我詐
道理說服不了
官就決定判令
為何不用紙和筆
處理簡易的申請

舊規革新
合乎意義　省時
無謂繼續
浪費金錢　資源
誓章說明
務實說清　抗辯
官作判斷
寫下頒令　指示
就此完結
這麼簡單
就是如此

20. 3 Minute Summons

The three-minute hearing proceeds
You are arguing with me as communication
Extended deadline for submission of documents
Or apply to amend the pleadings
Or add and delete parties
Or terminate the representation of clients
This simple request
Application
Does not require
A court appearance to defend the application

Why did both parties meet in person
Explain to the master
Like the way to survive in the harem
Often intrigues
Reasons cannot convince others
Master then grants an order
Why not use paper and pen
To handle such application at ease

Innovation of old rules
Meaningful and time-saving
No point in continuing
Waste of money   And resources
Affirmation describes
Explain pragmatically   And defend
Official judgment by master
Write down the order   And direction
That is it
So simple
That is it

20. 3 Minute Summons

時常讚美和為自己而自豪，
捕捉著你正在燃燒的火。

Always praise and proud to be
yourself, catching the fire you
have burnt.

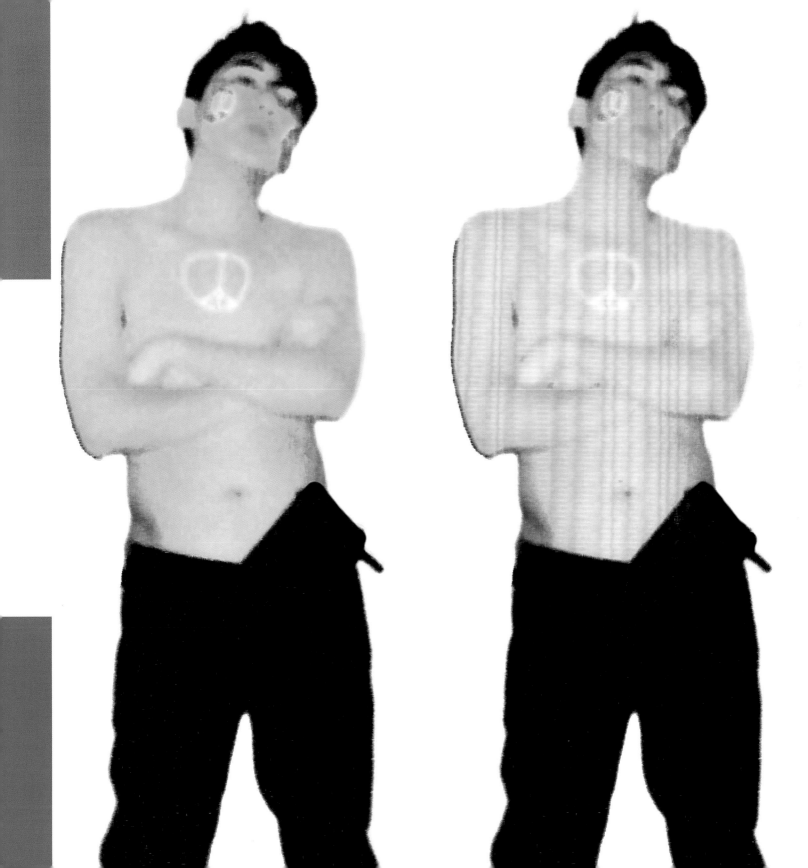

誰在意　　每天都有人走了
能抓住　　對的時候放光芒
困難過後　　忘掉昔日的難受
就像世人是善忘
在乎現在的安樂

逃離現實不能解決　　任何考驗
只用後悔換來不甘

街上人群　　一雙一對平常的事
也有些人　　獨身沒有伴侶一起
天意弄人　　從來不需去懷疑
渴望有人陪伴終老
生命就如此終結

家庭軼事　　有遺憾也有難忘事
陰晴圓缺　　人總要繼續行走著
到頭過來　　天終會計算好壞
是非也隨風塵散去
活過就無須回眸

南北方　　雖在同一個星球
千萬里　　距離拉遠歸屬感
像是獨處　　人之間總有隔膜
天空不常是晴朗
風雨不改是日常

曾經一起曾有緣份　　不是永恆
可不可惜視乎得失

在人日誌　　會紀錄發生什麼事
就算夢語　　在潛意識中為預知
執迷人事　　傷了身心皆難斷
解決的終解決不了
痴人說夢變瘋癲

別再度沈淪　　　也別再度空虛
有內心主角無限支持
有勇氣面對　　人生十常九事
也不過如此

放開胸襟　　經一事必會長一智
異觀奇蹟　　解釋不到當中奧妙
如果有幸　　將夢想變成真事
唱遊在那個桃源
歡樂盡興不終止

如果悉尼　　建一個迪士尼樂園
你我願此　　放低彼此心中瑣事
投入夢幻　　國度的每項設施
學習童話箇中意義
人生就確實如此

21.　如果悉尼有迪士尼樂園

Who cares   People leave every day
Can catch it   And shine when it's right
After the difficulty is over   Forget the pain of the past
Just like people in the world who are forgetful
Care about the present happiness

Escaping reality cannot solve   Any test
Only regret in exchange for unwillingness

Crowds of people on the street   Ordinary things like a couple
There are also people   Who are single without a partner
There is no need to doubt that   God wills his way
Longing for someone to accompany the other till old
Life ends like this

Family anecdotes   Have regrets and unforgettable moments
People always have to keep walking   When the clouds and sunshine fade away
In the end   God will calculate the good and the bad
Right and wrong also disperse with the wind and dust
Once you have lived there is no need to look back

North and South   Though are on the same planet
Thousands of miles away   Sense of belonging is far away
Like being alone   There is always a gap between people
The sky is not always clear
Rain or shine is the daily routine

We once had a fate together   It is not eternal
It's a pity which depends on the gain and loss

The in-person log   Will record what happened
Even if the dream language   Is precognition in the subconscious mind
Obsessing with love affairs   Hurts both body and mind and it is uneasy to break
What can't be solved will never be solved
Idiots talk about dreams and become extremely crazy

Don't wallow again   Don't be blankness again
There is unlimited support from the inner protagonist
Have the courage to face   The ten common things in life
Nothing more than that

Be open-minded   You will gain wisdom every time you experience something
Strange sights and miracles   Unable to explain the mystery
If you are lucky enough   Turing your dream into reality
Singing and playing in that paradise
The joy never ends

If Sydney   Built a Disneyland
You and I want this   To put aside the trivial matters in each other's hearts
Dive into every facility   In the dreamland
Learn the meaning of fairy tales
That's how life is

21. If Sydney Had A Disneyland

坐在海邊長椅
回想我他一起

他已在另天邊
告別在此應有的時間

活著訴說世途
窮貧分別人不再有深度
恐懼死亡佔大多數
因做太多傷害天理事務
每天有人離世上路
每天有新生接觸世間在開始領悟人定律知足
在燃燒理性心路

天上人間在何處
尋找不到走應該走的路
懷才不遇的人多數
就不能打破宿命願服輸

貪慕羨光燈下的霧
娛樂太多影響判斷力去選擇對或錯誤的劇目
讓邪惡入侵身體
千擁萬呼的造星群
在燃燒人理智在測驗羊群的心理利用找利益
在情緒起伏吸靈

人愈耀眼　　爬愈高終逃不過了命數
無人可見　　心不忿白活了一場
視而不見　　平淡地過生活　　理虧當前
誰告訴我　　他的一生　　就是借鏡

不安不樂不說
在沈默平靜大地去探索
高我他找到連繫多
維度不在限三維局限多
他看到過去和未來
告訴我眼前只是微塵不需在意好惡之爭煩擾
天在看人做什麼

人要覺醒不再沉倫
在人為居心下訊息干擾人的高智變人偶奴隸
物質與理性反比
心神不定被誰利用
沈默地去接受做奴隸去為了世一至尊去賣命
供養榮華給那群

因為驚恐　　是黑暗的食糧　　愈多滿足
因為貪婪　　天多灰不晴朗
人有選擇　　不能搪塞人事　　被迫犯罪
開始學習　　用心感應　　相信高我

22.　世途說

Sitting on a bench by the beach
Think of me and him together

He is already on the other side
Say goodbye to the time he deserved here

Live to tell the life journey theory
Poverty divides ones no longer have thorough judgment
Fear of death accounts for the majority
For doing too many harmful things immorally
Every day must have ones be died and taken to the road
Every day new infants come into contact with the world
—and begin to understand the laws of man and be contented
Burning rational roads of heart

Where is heaven and earth
Can't find the path I should take
Most people have talent but unlucky
If you can't break the fate you are willing to admit failure

Envy the fog under the light
Too much entertainment affects your judgment in choosing the right or wrong play
Let evil invade the body
The star-making group that is supported by thousands of people
Burning one's sanity testing the herd mentality and searching for interest
To absorb one's soul during his up and down of emotion

The more dazzling a person is
The higher he climbs but ultimately he cannot escape his fate
Seeing nobody   Being aggrieved for living a life in vain
Turn a blind eye   Live life indifferently   Make sense of the present
Who told me   His life   Is an example

Uneasy unhappy and speechless
Explore in the land of silence and tranquility
Higher self he finds more connections
Dimensions are not limited to three dimensions
He sees the past and the future
Tell me I'm just a mote of dust in front of me and don't worry about
—the disputes about goods and evils
God is watching what people do

People need to wake up and no longer be silent
The highly intelligent person who interferes with
-people's messages under artificial intentions becomes a puppet slave
Materiality and rationality are inversely proportional
Who is taking advantage of me when I am uneasy
To accept being a slave in silence
-and to sacrifice one's life for the supreme being
Offer glory to those people

Because fear
Is the food of darkness
The more satisfied you are
Because of greed
The sky is gray and not sunny
People have choices
Cannot prevaricate duty
And be forced to commit crimes
Start learning
To feel with your heart
And believe in your higher self

22. Life Journey Theory

從黑暗到光明是一個人類應該
學習並釋放自己的過程。

Darkness to Brightness is a
process of what a human being
should have learnt and free
himself/herself.

四面八方侵蝕我
傳媒在煽風點火
庸俗旋律　　當新潮衣　（沒有品味　　唱壞了調）
男生滿脂油粉面
女生暴露蕩樣兒
歌詞沒有新意思　　（重復幾千萬遍）
挑逗舞蹈又如何
俊朗樣子贏什麼
沒有歌喉是歌王　　（任何人也能勝任）
青黃不接告別盛年
沒有大將保留把持
樂壇還有什麼留戀　（婊子　　你說得對）

什麼頒獎禮
胡作非為當正事
背後暗中聽指示　　（潛在利益的風險）
音樂頒獎禮
難聽音樂多滿是
沒有資格來樹敵爭地　（慶典沒什麼意思）

狂迷全球皆是
去崇拜那些沒料知音
顯然那些人質數低
像吸毒思覺失調沈迷

沒有才華人捧頭
用美貌壟斷分數
洋洋得意覺得飛上頭　（已上位）
他人才華更出眾
可惜不被人看重
壞人挑壞人當道　（借偶像將黑變白）

天團已討厭
來自亞洲全世界
造星已不是未來的天
西洋黑娘子
蛇蠍美人的交易
狂迷愚昧墮落的逃避

供養這些怪物
痴漢婦瘋了心甘情願　　（錢多作怪）
不可否認昔日巨星
比現代造星高檔層次

什麼玩兒頒獎禮
領獎人自以為是
真的得到萬千的支持
懂得要將心比心
不要自欺騙自己
他根本什麼也都不是

往後人記不起
他稱帝稱后憑什麼事
知識都會長智
調子存在但憑空消失

誰是誰的歌曲
一首平庸歌不會流傳
昔日的經典不過時
因為真音樂大眾支持
（昔日稱帝稱后憑著真才本事）

浪費人作大志
傳媒不應再浪費報時
恥笑多於欣賞幼稚
頒獎禮繼續渾水摸魚

世一絕對不是
這現代不知所謂寵兒
（不會理會這些已腐爛的小圈子）
不被虐我理智
只視昔日崇高標誌

23. 頒獎禮

Attacking me from all sides
The media is fanning the flames
Vulgar melody   Used as fashionable clothes   (No taste   Sing with a bad tune)
Boys wear too many make up
Girls expose their slutty looks
The lyrics have no new meaning   (Repeated tens of millions of times)
So what about provocative dancing
What does one win by looking handsome
Can be a singer without singing talent   (Anyone can do it)
Farewell to the prime of life
No real talented ones remain to take control
Not worth to love the music industry   (Bitch   you're right)

What award ceremony
Doing wrong is the right thing to do
Taking instructions secretly   (Risk of potential benefits)
Music award ceremony
So much bad music
You are not qualified to make enemies and compete in that industry   (Celebrations are not meaningful)

Fans everywhere in the world
Worship for those untalented friends
Apparently those people are of low quality
Like drug addiction mental disorder to obsess

One who has no talent to praise
Use beauty to monopolize points
Feeling so proud that they are flying to the top   (Already on top)
Others are more talented
It's a pity that no one takes them seriously
The bad guys pick the bad guys as the mainstream   (Use idols to turn black into white)

Top bands I already hate them
From Asia and the world
Star-making is no longer hot in the future
Western black lady
Femme fatale deal
The escape from the fever fans' madness ignorance and depravity

Feed these monsters
Crazy men and insane women are willing to go crazy   (Too much money causes trouble)
It's undeniable that those former superstars
Are at higher level than modern manmade stars

What does an award ceremony plays for
The award recipients are self-righteous
Really think they get thousands of support
Know how to put one's heart into another's heart
Don't deceive yourself
He is nothing at all

No one in the future will be able to remember
What do ones do after they proclaim themselves as kings or queens
Knowledge will make you wise
The tone exists but vanishes into air

Whose song
A mediocre song will not spread
Classics from the past never outdated
Because real music is supported by the mass
(In the past when ones became kings or queens they relied on their true talents)
A waste of people's ambition
The media should no longer waste time reporting
Ridicule more than appreciate childishness
The award ceremony continues to slack off

To be the top is definitely not
All those nonsense darlings in this modern world
(Ignore these rotten small coteries)
I am not abused I am rational
Only serving the icons in the past as the top

23. Award Ceremony

獨自逛遊台北的市城　　顯得孤獨得很
旅伴從來沒有　　自己成行
不強求別人施捨憐憫　　陪我完成旅程
多年一個人旅遊廣見聞
享受一個人　　天大地天　　逍遙任行
偶爾想擁有　　理想同伴　　喔....

其實我不介意分開各自尋樂
短暫在一起共同逛吃喝
分享遊記嶄新經歷　　能不能
既然不一起同樂在每個旅行
不要奢望我會買些手信
但到最後　　想分享樂　　總有禮成

誠品書店早上的景觀　　人來往少得很
只看到一些老少在打轉
身邊忽然擦身一個人　　背著背包的人
他在尋覓他需要的書本
我有我精神　　放慢步看興趣的作品
找到一本書　　叫緣來愛在

原來他在尋找這本書除疑問
我手中拿著他需要慰藉天燈
恰巧一本割愛讓他　　能不能　　喔....
我不介意成全他認真的純真
他感激我的率真與天真
言語一致　　他也獨自　　漫遊市城

偶然相識一個素未謀面的人
在書店咖啡店談笑風生
感覺彷如心靈的旅伴　　輕鬆很
離開台北客機中遇見他坐乘
緣份就在此萌愛念而生
我們愛情　　隨意展開　　侶伴終生

24.　在台北誠品書店遇見愛情

Walking around the city of Taipei Alone   It seems very lonely
Never have Travel companions   Travel by myself
Don't force others to show mercy   To accompany me on my journey
Traveling alone for many years and gaining extensive knowledge
Enjoy being alone   In the sky and the earth   Free and easy
Sometimes I want to have   An ideal companion   Oh....

Actually I don't mind having fun separately
Spend a short time eating and drinking together
Share new travel experience with each other   Can or cannot
Since we don't have fun together on every trip
Don't expect me to buy some souvenirs
But in the end   I want to share the joy   There will always be gifts for courtesy

The scenery of Eslite Bookstore in the morning   Very few people there
I just saw some old and young people spinning around
Suddenly a person passed by me   A person carrying a backpack
He was looking for the books he needs
I had my own spirit   I took my time and read the works that interest me
Found a book   And it was titled as The Fate of Love is Here

It turns out he was looking for this book to clear up his doubts
I held the sky lantern in my hand that he needed comfort
There was only once copy coincidently to give it to him   Could or could not   Oh....
I did not mind fulfilling his serious innocence
He appreciated my frankness and innocence
Our language was consistent   He was alone   To roam the city

Accidental acquaintance with someone you have never met before
Chatting and laughing in the bookstore and coffee shop
Feeling like a spiritual travel companion   Very relaxed
I met him on the passenger plane leaving Taipei
Fate was born from this cute thought of love
Our love   Unfolding at will   And we are partners for life

24. Meeting Love At Eslite Bookstore In Taipei

從小被灌輸當律師醫生會計師
精算建築師當成功人士
在社會受尊敬有高尚的價值　（價值）

從小被人督促成績要名列前茅
不斷的考試存在那鬥志
叫人羨慕被寵愛當個好孩子　（好孩子）

完美　人從來不會完美　　（完美）　Hoo....
社會　向來是比較勢利　　（勢利）

帶我走　　　奔向自由
不由自主難以得承受
燃亮我　　　不羈的風
我要打開心扉去獲得
那自由
Or Or Or Or Or　　Or Or Ar　Or Or Or Oh　（相信）
愛自由
Or Or Or Or Or　　Or Or Ar　Or Or Or Oh　（自己）

媽媽的話聽得多永不錯真的
爸爸精神虐待著我繁多
造成昨天的我受盡心理折磨

Or　Or Or Or　Or　Or Or
Or　Or Or Or　Or　Or Or

我靜靜哭了被冷漠　（冷漠）
每次　　只有內心給安慰　　（安慰）

要振作　　枷鎖擺脫
不要再受爸媽的委托
那工作　　不能愛多
浪費青春是出賣的禍
我失落
Or Or Or Or Or　　Or Or Ar　Or Or Or Oh　（堅持）
不快樂
Or Or Or Or Or　　Or Or Ar　Or Or Or Oh　（信念）

萬劫不復困在那囚室
用權利物質威脅我
如你愛我別再管束我
放手讓我自由高飛
Set Me Free

愛創作　　那個是我
不需擔心碰撞血破
如快樂　　找對的多
承受不比現在的多
放開我
Set me free

Or Or Or Or Or　　Or Or Ar　Or Or Or Oh　（無怨）
我的路是獨特
我看起我
Or Or Or Or Or　　Or Or Ar　Or Or Or Oh　（無悔）
別要求你的我
不要理我
Or Or Or Or Or　　Or Or Ar　Or Or Or Oh　（發射）
你要支持著我
長大的我
Or Or Or Or Or　　Or Or Ar　Or Or Or Oh　（光芒）

25. Free Me

Since I was small I was nurtured to be a lawyer doctor accountant
Actuary architect and to be a successful person
To be respected and had noble value in society   (Value)

Since I was small I was urged to be the top in academics
Constant examinations let that fighting spirit existed
Admired by others and pet as being a good child (Good child)

Perfect   Humans are never perfect all along   (Perfect) Hoo....
Society   Always be comparably snobbish   (Snobbish)

Take me away   Running to freedom
Never be yourself is hard to bear
Light me up   Unruly wind
I need to open my heart to acquire
That freedom
Or Or Or Or Or   Or Or Ar Or Or Or Oh   (Believe)
Or Or Or Or Or   Or Or Ar Or Or Or Oh   (Myself)

Hearing lost of mama's words is not wrong really
Papa psychologically abused me a lot
Causing me of the past being psychologically tortured without an end

Or Or Or Or Or Or Or
Or Or Or Or Or Or Or

I cried quietly for being indifferent (Indifferent)
Every time   Only my heart comforts me   (Comfort)

Need to cheer up   Get rid of shackles
Don't be appointed and directed by your Papa and Mama again
That job   Can't love more
Wasting youth is the scourge of betrayal
I desperate
Or Or Or Or Or   Or Or Ar Or Or Or Oh (Insist)
Unhappy
Or Or Or Or Or   Or Or Ar Or Or Or Oh (Faith)

Being Irreversibly trapped in that prison
Threatening me with the right interest and material
If you love me don't control me
Leave your hands and let me fly highly and freely
Set Me Free

Love creative production   That's me
No need to worry
If happy   Finding a lot right
A lot to bear now is similar as the past
Set me free

Or Or Or Or Or   Or Or Ar Or Or Or Oh (No complaint)
My road is unique
I look at me
Or Or Or Or Or   Or Or Ar Or Or Or Oh_ (No regret)
Don't demand that I am yours
Don't bother me
Or Or Or Or Or   Or Or Ar Or Or Or Oh (Emission)
You have to support me
I grow up
Or Or Or Or Or   Or Or Ar Or Or Or Oh (Light)

25. Free Me

儘管有時大霧
我都能看清楚
雨中之下跳舞
不會美中不足
勤奮完成拼圖
一汗一滴堆土
為了下代安逸
不計較那辛苦
土生土長無數
代代相傳滿足
一步一生清楚
為誰奉獻清楚
精英頻出威武
工業金融科技
創意無限商機
人才濟濟一起

香港
這是個美好的地方
這就是香港

漁港變成都市
百年艱業發展
東方之珠美艷
國際重要樞紐
種族混合生活
和諧沒有歧視
東西美食匯集
時尚沒有界限
市民安居樂業
交通方便快捷
時間沒有停止
媒體五花百門
節目滔滔不絕
話題天天新意
緊貼資訊時事

香港
這是個繁榮的地方
這就是香港

山頂居高臨下
維港夜色無邊
四季氣候佳宜
新戲日日上演
紅館伊館博覽館
演唱會放送不完
演藝文化中心
劇目不需懷疑
得到大佛普照
大澳留住自然
赤柱海洋公園
荔園令人懷念
酒樓飲食文化
人人不能幸免
魚蛋砵糕腸粉
確實令人懷念

回歸後的年月
人和地不斷在變遷
每個歷史人都見證著
風浪大小到底不算是什麼
Ei Yeah Er Er Er Yeah
Ei Yeah Er Er Er Yeah

不朽傳世下去
因為
這就是
香港

香港人
放鬆一下
繼續微笑
發熱發亮永不停止
這就是香港
正能量傳送不息
獅子山下
你我都傳承那精神
不朽傳世下去
因為
這就是
香港

26. 香港

Although sometimes foggy
I can see clearly
Dancing under the rain
No imperfection
Working hard to complete the puzzle
Every drop of sweat to pile up the soil
For the comfort of the next generation
Don't care about the hard work
Numerous natives
Satisfaction passed on from generation to generation
Clear one step at a time
Clear for whom to contribute
Elites frequently appear mighty
Industrial Fintech
Unlimited creative business opportunities
Talents come together

Hong Kong
This is a wonderful place
This is Hong Kong

Fishing port turns into a city
Hundred years of hard work development
The Pearl of the Orient
Important international hub
Mixing of races to live
Harmony without discrimination
East and West Food Collection
No boundaries for fashion
Citizens live and work in peace and contentment
Convenient and fast transportation
Time doesn't stop
Media of all kinds
The show is endless
New topics every day
Keep up with information and current affairs

Hong Kong
This is a prosperous place
This is Hong Kong

Condescending on the top of the mountain
No boundary for the night of Victoria Harbour
Good weather in all seasons
New plays are staged every day
Hong Kong Coliseum Queen Elizabeth Stadium Asia Expo
Concert will be never ending
Performing arts and cultural centers
The play are extremely exciting
With protection of the Buddha Statue
Tai O keeps nature
Disneyland Ocean Park
Lai Yuen is nostalgic
Restaurant food culture
Everyone is not immune
Fish ball Steamed rice cake and steamed Vermicelli roll
Really nostalgic

After reunification for many years and months
People and places are constantly changing
Everyone in history has witnessed
It does not matter how strong the wind and the wave are
Ei Yeah Er Er Er Yeah
Ei Yeah Er Er Er Yeah

Hong Kong people
Relax for a moment
Keep smiling
Never stop to heat and shine
This is Hong Kong
Positive energy is transmitted endlessly
Under the Lion Rock
You and I both inherit that spirit
Immortality passed down from generation to generation
Because
This is
Hong Kong

26. Hong Kong

人活最後終離場
回到大自然路上
合上雙眼後
看不到人無常

世上存在過
忘記是平常
露水不乏味
光影不留長

回到最清澈
新鮮的氣味
踏上社會之初
有苦有甜不時回味

青春無限的空氣內
美好期盼著未來
擁有誰　　愛上誰
不陷入深海
活在浪漫的年代
最簡單的愛
聽見了誰　　看過誰
充斥著腦袋

互勵互勉說真話
縱然有時會孤立
無情的人群
不為誰打圓場

年青的朝氣
鬥志會延長
不怕輸給誰
站立重新出發

忘掉了所失
憧憬著最美
青春的臉容下
沒殘留那動人倉疤

青春無限的空氣內
美好期盼著未來
擁有誰　　愛上誰
不陷入深海
活在浪漫的年代
最簡單的愛
聽見了誰　　看過誰
充斥著腦袋

但活在青春空氣內
呼吸不怎麼有害
愛過誰　　幫過誰
不會有更改
成人污漳的世界內
充斥著無盡感既
年青無罪　　是最美
純真的年代

27.　年青無罪

People must leave the world at the end
Back to the road of nature
After closing their eyes
Can't see impermanence

Existed in the world
Forgetting is normal
Dew is not boring
Light and shadow do not stay long

Back to the green and astringency
Fresh smell
Stepping at the beginning of society
Aftertaste the bitterness and sweetness from time to time

In the infinite youthful air
Looking forward to the future
Who have possessed   Who have been loved
Not plunge into the deep sea
Living in a romantic age
The simplest love
Who have heard   Who have seen
Full of head

Mutual encouragement to tell the truth
Even though sometimes will be isolated
Ruthless crowd
Not for anyone to end the show

Youthful vitality
Fighting spirit will be extended
Not afraid to lose to whom
Stand up and start again

Forget about the loss
Looking forward to the most beautiful
Under the youthful face
Without leaving that moving scars

In the infinite youthful air
Looking forward to the future
Who have possessed   Who have been loved
Not plunge into the deep sea
Living in a romantic age
The simplest love
Who have heard   Who have seen
Full of head

But living in the air of youth
Breathing is not very harmful
Who have loved   Who have helped
No changes
In the polluted adult world
Full of endless feeling
Being young is innocent   Is the most beautiful
Age of Innocence

27. Young Is Innocent

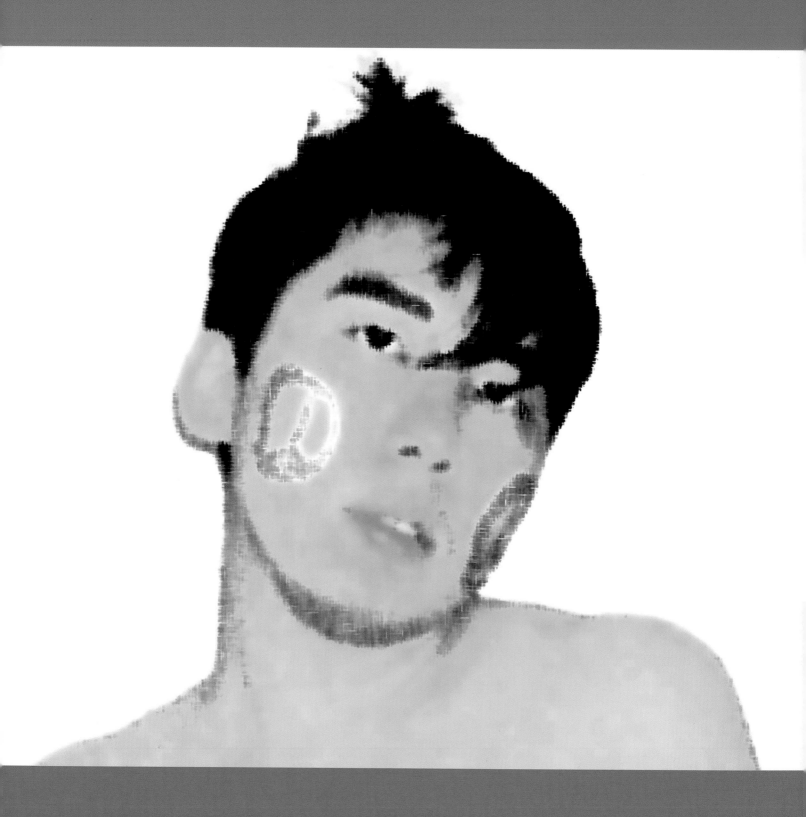

一個人　　兩個人
都是根據那劇本
誰在位　　誰篡位
歷史輪轉不陌生
太多諷刺視頻
太多陰謀神論
我望著荷李活山想像

給我一大束花朵
心情開放快樂
不被那負力量擋阻
人真會明白麼
享受舞曲的節奏
舞著是力量
遊戲沒有真正完結
世道說

不管人怎樣　　我懂得去愛我
不隨波逐流　　不受媒體擺唆

時代過　　一個個
沒有絕對的旋律
用物質　　牢住人
愛用富貧作勝負
她高調去炫耀
他為名利盲目
最後獨終帶不走一切

戰亂名牌是什麼
海嘯錢幣沒了
缺糧加密幣不用
人還不明白麼

就算世界有末日
貪嗔癡所累
是人為力量作一切
或許是自然的法則
誰判斷

人在做天在看　　誰是對誰是錯
誰不自愛墮落　　誰為利益犯錯
誰出賣了靈魂　　誰入端正大道
誰會一敗塗地　　誰為正義得道
誰是心存好念　　把持

沒有生命殘缺　　沒有後悔不屑
沒有賣弄權力交錯線

是時候告別物質
走向心靈境界
昇華到五度空間
沒有慾望概念
不用作任何的表情
神交是一切
沒有人為名利爭鬥
金錢不再是交易點
世改變

沒有名店樹立　　再沒有暴發戶
沒有星光熠熠　　不需視聽娛樂
沒有貧窮懸殊　　沒有高費消遣
沒有嫉惡如仇　　沒有階級觀念
只有心靈開竅　　正面

28. 告別物質 走向心靈

One person   Two people
It's all based on that script
Who is in power   Who usurped the throne
The cycle of history is not strange
Too many sarcastic videos
Too many conspiracy theories
I look at Hollywood Hills and imagine

Give me a bouquet of flowers
Feeling of open and happy
Don't be blocked by that negative force
Do people really understand
Enjoy the rhythm of dance music
Dancing is power
The game is not really over
Experience tells

No matter who I am   I know how to love me
Don't follow the crowd   Don't be instigated by the media

Time passed   One by one
No absolute melody
Use substances   To hold people firmly
Love to win or lose with rich and poor
She shows off in high profile
He is blind for fame
In the end alone can't take everything away

What are famous brands stand for in chaotic wars
Coins are gone in tsunami
Food shortage cryptocurrency no need
People still don't understand
Even if the world ends
Tired of greed hatred and ignorance
It's human power that does everything
Perhaps it is the law of nature
Who judges

Man is doing what the sky is watching   Who is right and who is wrong
Who doesn't love himself and degenerates   Who makes mistakes for profit
Who sold his soul   Who entered the righteous way
Who will fail   Who will win for justice
Who is holding goodness in heart   Keeping forward

No loss of life   No regrets and disdain
No show off power staggered lines

It's time to say goodbye to material things
Heading to the spiritual realm
Sublimating to the five dimensional space
No concept of desire
No need to show any facial expression
God is everything
No one fights for fame
Money is no longer the point of exchange
The world changes

No famous stores established   No more upstarts
No star-studded   No audio-visual entertainment
No poverty disparity   No high-cost entertainment
No enmity   No concept of classes
Only the mind is enlightened   Be Positive

28. Bid Farewell To The Material Going To The Soul

Ooo Ooo Ooo Ooo Ooh
Ooo Ooo Ooo Ooo Ooh
（我讓你著迷）
Ooo Ooo Ooo Ooo Ooh
（我有我魅力）
Ooo Ooo Ooo Ooo Ooh
（因為我是婊子）

我有性格就不用你來解讀什麼
我不喜歡的過去有梵文那麼多
我曾經想過永遠記住我的仇人
我幻想過生活在鎂光閃耀當中

我有承受過了什麼
哪有爭取了真快樂
哭了有人會理會麼
沒有名利又算什麼

拼命搏　　人之過
羨慕他人擁有多
同年紀百萬年薪
La La La La La
沒有錢　　沒拍拖
過了年青得什麼
孤獨潦倒失敗多
Bitch I am Gawan

婊子　　那就是我
婊子　　一定是我

為何羨慕妒忌他人富貴地生活
為何要為利名去委屈埋沒自我
快樂在心很簡單不需物質襯托
為何不能自主圍繞別人去生活

不愛虛偽空話的人
不愛利益主義的人
不愛炫耀無品的人
Ooo Ooo Ooo Ooh
不愛慢拍固執的人
（無法走近）

Bitch Gawan Go

努力只有我知道
外人看我輕鬆活
諷刺我多麼快樂
La La La La La
別人誤解我很多
沒條件自主地過
祈求命運會大轉
Bitch I am Gawan

婊子　　那就是我
婊子　　一定是我

不愛自私瘋癲的人
不愛無同理心的人
Ooo Ooo Ooo Ooh
不愛阿諛奉承的人
（無法走近）

不能討好每人
更不能討好全世界
那只好討好自己
不需聽人說三道四
我犯過錯　　不會往後過
因我是婊子　　不是聖人
隨波逐流　　不是我層次
隨心而所欲　　我就是贏家
率真隨性是表現
音樂電影重要
感性流露表現
男女異性同性相戀
思想開放自如
找代母去產子
不是苟且之事
不愛 overated
驕女韓團鏡子
表裡不一偽善
才華人造理念
玩具是我心智
律師從不是我的大志
移民遺產土地
有興趣去投資
不愛虛幣金融
個個不務正業
橫財一朝喪智
正財是我概念
食傷是我標籤
玩具過萬百千
代理品牌開店
開博物館咖啡店展示

迪士尼樂園
選我做高層或永遠大使
做迪士尼的狂熱份子
不是一朝一夕的事
建立潮流品牌創業
出版文曲專輯影響世界
樂於做個永恆的傳記婊子

九運利紅又利火
我缺火水多之禍
迎來最佳的生活
La la La La La
認識你　　認識我
千財萬貫又如何
追求心靈的平和
Bitch I am Gawan

Ooo Ooo Ooo Ooo Ooh
（不會有後悔）
Ooo Ooo Ooo Ooo Ooh
（不需去澄清）
Ooo Ooo Ooo Ooo Ooh
（不需去動怒）
Ooo Ooo Ooo Ooo Ooh
（因我是婊子）

你認為你是誰
（因我是婊子）
你認為他是誰
（他只是痞子）
你認為她是誰（她是個混蛋）
我就是個婊子

做婊子抑或做混蛋
I am Gawan the Bitch....
and that is

29. Bitch I Am Gawan!

Ooo Ooo Ooo Ooo Ooh
Ooo Ooo Ooo Ooo Ooh
(I fascinate you)
Ooo Ooo Ooo Ooo Ooh
(I have my charm)
Ooo Ooo Ooo Ooo Ooh
(Because I'm a bitch)

I have my character so I don't need you to interpret it
Things about the past that I don't like as many as Sanskrit
I once wanted to remember my enemy forever
I imagined living in the spotlight

What have I endured
How can I be really happy if I strive for it
Will anyone care if I cry
What's nothing without fame and fortune

Fight hard   It's human fault
Envy others who have so much
Annual salary of one million dollars for the same age
La La La La La
No money   No date
What do you get when I am young
Lonely down and out there are many failures
Bitch I am Gawan

Bitch   That's me
Bitch   It must be me

Why we have to admire and envy other people's wealthy lives
Why should we suffer and bury ourselves for the sake of fame and gain
Happiness in the heart is very simple and does not require material support
Why can't we live our lives around others on our own

Don't love people who are hypocritical and empty talk
Don't like people interest-seeking
Don't like people show off and have no taste
Ooo Ooo Ooo Ooh
Don't like stubborn people with slow pace
(Cannot get closer)

Bitch Gawan Go

Only I know the hard work
Outsiders think I live an easy life
Irony how happy I am
La La La La La
Others misunderstand me a lot
Live independently without conditions
Pray that fate will change
Bitch I am Gawan
Bitch   That's me
Bitch   It must be me

Don't love selfish and crazy people
Don't love people who don't have empathy
Ooo Ooo Ooo Ooh
Don't like flatterers
(Cannot get closer)

Even can't please the whole world
Then I have to please myself
No need to listen to other people's gossip
I've made mistakes   I won't look back on them
Because I'm a bitch   Not a saint
Go with the flow   It's not my level
Do whatever I want   I'm the winner
Frankness and spontaneity are manifestations
Musical movies are important
Emotional expression
Heterosexual and homosexual love
Open-minded and comfortable
Find a surrogate mother to give birth
It's not a matter of persuasion
Dislike those being overated
Top Girl Korean Group Mirror
Duplicity and hypocrisy
Talent man-made concept
The toy is my mind
Being a lawyer was never my ambition
Immigration probate and lands
Interested in investing
Don't like virtual currency and finance
Everyone is not doing their job properly
A sudden fortune will make you lose your mind
Constant wealth is my concept
Using my talent to get wealth is my label

Hundreds and thousands of toys
Open a store as an agent for a brand
Open a museum coffee shop to display
Disneyland
Appoint me as a senior executive or permanent ambassador
Be a Disney super fan
It's not something that happens overnight
Establish a trendy brand and start a business
Publish word song albums to influence the world
Happy to be an eternal biography bitch

Ninth Periods love red and ease for fire
I am short of fire with plenty of water
Welcome my best life
La la La La La
Knowing you   Knowing me
So what if I have a lot of wealth
Pursue peace of mind
Bitch I am Gawan

Ooo Ooo Ooo Ooo Ooh
(No regrets)
Ooo Ooo Ooo Ooo Ooh
(No need to clarify)
Ooo Ooo Ooo Ooo Ooh
(No need to rage)
Ooo Ooo Ooo Ooo Ooh
(Because I'm a bitch)

Who do you think you are
(Because I'm a bitch)
Who do you think he is
(He is just a ruffian)
Who do you think she is
(She's an asshole)
That is I'm a bitch

Be a bitch or be a jerk
I am Gawan the Bitch.... and that is

29. Bitch I Am Gawan!

關於 基宏 About Gawan

基宏是香港、澳洲及紐西蘭律師，也是一名作家、繪畫師及玩具精品收藏家。他自 1997 年起便開始繪畫人像，並於 2001 年起開始創作多首文曲，即以歌詞及新詩為體本的隨意創作文體。他於 2021 年 7 月首次在台灣出版首本實驗性質的文曲書本專輯「Who's That Virgin? He is.... Gawanlo」，並於 2024 年 7 月出版第一本正式的文曲書本專輯 「Virgin 處子」。

他喜歡自由創意，著重生活態度、文化時尚藝術及傳播資訊。他從不隨波逐流，不愛一切拘謹且守舊通俗的理念和概念。他認為人生不應只為追求物質而盲目消費自己的身心，應該善待自己和享受簡單的生活。他喜歡聆聽別人的故事和經歷及體會社會和生活上的不同文化和點滴，並希望透過所創作的作品令世人得以回歸簡單自然、宣揚愛與和平、重新認識自己和滴化心靈。

Gawan is a Hong Kong, Australian and New Zealand lawyer, a writer, a painter and a toy and accessory collector. He began painting portraits in 1997, and in 2001 he began to compose a number of word songs, a casual style of writing based on the format of lyrics and modern poetry. He published his first experimental word song book album titled "Who's That Virgin? He is.... Gawanlo" in Taiwan in July 2021, and published his first official word song book album titled "Virgin" in July 2024.

He likes free creativity and focuses on life attitude, culture, fashion, arts and dissemination of information. He never follows the trend and does not like all rigid and conservative ideas and concepts. He believes that life should not blindly consume one's body and only mind for material things, but should treat oneself well and enjoy a simple life. He likes to listen to other people's stories and experiences and embody different cultures and matters in society and life. He hopes that through the works he creates, people can return to simplicity and nature, promote love and peace, reunderstand themselves and transform their souls spiritually.

後記

在香港做了 10 多年律師，從來沒帶給我任何滿足感，因為我對法律的興趣始終不是最熱切。雖然我知道自己的興趣是藝術創作、文藝創作及設計，但人生就是這樣，年輕的時候往往因為天時、地理、人和而事與願違，沒有選擇的餘地。律師的生涯確實沒有帶給我很多好處，無論是經濟、人脈和成就等等。可能我不喜愛虛偽、花天酒地或野心勃勃地參與及出席眾多商界聯誼組織和活動，覺得這是刻意、造作及沒有什麼意思。

雖然律師不是我喜愛的職業，我卻沒有很厭惡的感覺。我很喜愛處理土地樓宇買賣、知識產權、信托、遺產及精神無行為能力等相關法律的文書和案件，因為藉此接觸到不同階層社會背景的人士、了解不同的人格甚至不同的生活習慣和方式，人情冷暖感受最深。另外，也愛做家庭協意及平安三寶，因為人不只要在生前為自己及家人負責，也要做一個負責人的死人，不能為最親或下一代為了自己生前的資產來怨恨悲傷。其實，人生的盡頭就是死亡，就算一個人享有無盡的榮華富貴，到頭來也像乞丐一樣死後什麼也帶不了，化塵入土，與親友緣盡離開人間往生，接受審判上天下地獄或進入六度輪迴。

2001 年，在葉勇博士的課堂下，我首次接觸到新詩或現代詩的創作。2019 年為了一嘗作家夢，我特意在當年 12 月中台北旅行中聯繫當地出版社，親見負責人士開會討論籌備出書事宜。我在此很感激白象文化的張輝潭老師及城邦文化的顏嘉慧老師。我還記得與張輝潭老師在台北車站的一間咖啡店暢談了約一小時，彼此交流了對文藝創作的心得，以及聆聽他累積的經驗及意見，令我好像上了一次寶貴的課堂。至於顏嘉慧老師，我感激她對我的不離不棄，半年內百多封電郵溝通不厭其煩在所不計，她耐心地指導我由零開始到我懂得排版及符合所需要求使我尊敬她的認真和耐性，此世也不能忘記她的大恩大德。其實，我也算很幸運，在恰巧下遇到這兩位在我文藝創作的啟蒙老師。另外，我感謝洪怡欣女士協助我與張輝潭老師的聯繫，也很多謝翁桂敏老師給予我中肯的意見及宣傳的配合，雖然最終未能成事，但也十分感激。

【Who's That Virgin? He is.... Gawanlo】 是我 2021 年 7 月在台灣出版的首本文曲書本專輯。由於我當年的心態是玩票性質，也沒什麼經驗，沒有考慮市場方向，也沒有任何宣傳，所以無人問曉。儘管如此，它也有存在的權利和價值，因為每一首文曲都是本人創作，紀錄了每一種心情、主題和表達的情感和意思，對我的成長或經驗都頗重要。另外，我不是名人或人氣明星，也不是被邀出書，能夠全力掌控書本封面、內容及設計，我感到很滿足。

因法律工作、生活及心情影響，加上財務資源的枷鎖，我放低了文藝創作約 2 年多，一直到 2023 年秋季開始，突然有種強烈的感覺喚起我創作的意欲，覺得是時候作轉變及真正展開文藝創作及其他喜歡的事業。

對於文藝創作的宗旨，我希望透過每一首文曲與讀者作最率真和直接的溝通及交流，各自對此有獨特的解讀。此外，也希望能舉辦現場研討會分享各自想法作直接互動及聆聽別人的經歷故事，為他們創作紀錄及大同分享。至於我對文藝創作的期望，希望我的文藝創作打破言語障礙，最終能征服及影響全世界的人，不分膚色，為他們帶來啓思及滴化心靈，令彼此的生活及社會充滿愛、和平及有意義。

我是一個感性的人，可能聽完一首歌、看完一套電影、一套電視劇及一場舞台劇或歌劇，也可能在社會、工作及生活上往往衍生無窮無盡的靈感，在喜怒哀樂的情緒中用文字紀錄每一刻的感覺。特別在寧靜無擾的深夜，是我最享受寫作的時間，也較能創作自我滿足及滿意的作品。有些文曲作品是我的體會、經歷和心聲，有些是寫別人的故事，有些是寫社會生活，也有些是天馬行空的幻想主題。　無論怎樣，文藝創作是我最真實及最佳的構通橋樑，也為我生存在世上作一個紀錄，能夠不受時限留存。

除了文藝創作外，有人問我有還有什麼夢想。坦白說，我願望能開一間屬於自己的工作室、一間玩具博物館、一間主題茶店、一間含代理玩具、食品及健康產品的公司、一間出版社和一間表演藝術及演唱會製作公司等等。此外，也希望由於我是超級迪士尼迷，如果能委任為迪士尼樂園全球永遠榮譽大使，真是功德完滿。

每個人心中的一團火儘管時亮時弱，但總不能熄滅。因為，夢想是生存之源，能否達成旨在能夠持久努力及堅持。至於我之後的人生，交給上天順其自然的去吧，我相信大家充滿正能量，簡化生活的事，知足且安份，不傷害別人和自己，一定會走得愈來愈好。

最後，但願得到廣大讀者的喜愛與支持，能夠繼續出版不同主題的文曲書本專輯，分享你我他的生活態度、難忘經歷和動人故事。

基宏

Epilogue

Working as a lawyer in Hong Kong for more than 10 years has never given me any sense of satisfaction because my interest in law has never been the most fervent. Although I know that my interests are artistic creation, literary creation and design, life is like this. When I was young, things often backfired because of the timing, geography, and people relations, and I had no choice. A career as a lawyer has indeed not brought me many benefits, whether it is financial, connections, achievements, etc. Maybe I don't like hypocrisy, debauchery, or ambitious participation in and attendance at many business networking organizations and activities. I think it is deliberate, artificial and meaningless.

Although being a lawyer is not my favorite profession, I don't feel very disgusted with it. I really enjoy working on legal documents and cases related to conveyancing, intellectual property, trust, probate and mental incapacity, because through this I can get in touch with people from different social backgrounds, understand different personalities and even different living habits and styles, and I can feel the warmth and indifference of human nature the most. In addition, I also like to make family agreements and the three instruments of peace, because people not only have to be responsible for themselves and their families during life, but also have to be a responsible person after death. They cannot grieve for their closest relatives or the next generation for their own assets' disputes during life. In fact, the end of life is death. Even if a person enjoys endless glory and wealth, in the end he will be like a beggar with nothing to take with him after death. He will turn into dust and die, leave his relatives and friends, and pass away. He will be judged and go to heaven and hell or enter the six degrees of reincarnation.

In 2001, I was exposed to the creation of new poetry or modern poetry for the first time in Dr. Yip Yung's classes. In order to fulfill my dream of being a writer in 2019, I deliberately contacted the local publishing house during my trip to Taipei in mid-December of that year and witnessed the responsible persons meeting to discuss preparations for publishing a book. I am very grateful to Mr. Zhang Huitan of Elephant White Cultural Enterprise Co. Ltd and Ms. Yan Jiahui of Cite Publishing Limited. I still remember chatting with Mr. Zhang Huitan for about an hour in a coffee shop at Taipei Station. We exchanged ideas on literary and artistic creation, and listened to his accumulated experience and opinions. It felt like I had received a valuable class. As for Ms. Yan Jiahui, I am grateful for her persistence in me. She went through hundreds of emails in half a year without bothering to communicate. She patiently guided me from scratch until I knew how to design and edit the layout and meet all relevant requirements. I respect her seriousness and patience, her great kindness will never be forgotten in this life. In fact, I am very lucky to have met these two enlightening teachers who inspired me in my literary and artistic creation. In addition, I am grateful to Ms. Hong Yixin for assisting me in contacting Mr. Zhang Huitan, and I am also grateful to Ms. Weng Guimin for giving me pertinent opinions and cooperation in publicity. Although it did not happen in the end, I am very grateful.

[Who's That Virgin? He is.... Gawanlo] is my first book album of literary works published in Taiwan in July 2021. Because at that time I was just for fun, I had no experience, I didn't consider the market, and I didn't have any publicity, so no one knew about it. Despite this, it also has the right and value to exist, because every word song was written by me and recorded every mood, theme, emotion and meaning expressed. It is very important to my growth or experience. In addition, I am not a celebrity or popular star, nor have I been invited to publish a book. I feel very satisfied that I can fully control the cover, content and design of the book.

Due to the influence of my legal work, life and mood, as well as the shackles of financial resources, I put down my literary and artistic creation for about two years. Until the beginning of the autumn of 2023, I suddenly had a strong feeling that aroused my desire to create, and I felt that it was time to expose my creativity, transform and truly develop my writing career and other favorite undertakings.

Regarding the purpose of literary and artistic creation, I hope to have the most candid and direct communication with readers through each word song, and each of them will have a unique interpretation of this. In addition, I also hope to hold a live show to share each other's ideas for direct interaction and listen to other people's stories, creating records for them and sharing them together. As for my expectations, I hope that my literary and artistic creation can break the language barrier and eventually conquer and influence people all over the world, regardless of races, bring them inspiration and transform their hearts, and fill each other's lives and society with love, peaceful and meaningful.

I am an emotional person. I may listen to a song, watch a movie, a TV series, a drama or an opera, or I may often derive endless inspiration in society, work and life. Use words to record the feelings of each moment in the emotions of sadness and joy. Especially in the quiet and undisturbed late night, this is the time when I enjoy writing the most, and I am more able to create works that are self-satisfying. Some word songs are my experiences, experiences and thoughts, some are about other people's stories, some are about social life, and some are about fantasy themes. No matter what, literary and artistic creation is the truest and best bridge for me to connect, and it also creates a record of my life in the world that can be preserved without time limit.

In addition to literary and artistic creation, someone asked me what other dreams I have. Frankly speaking, I hope to open a studio of my own, a toy museum, a theme tea shop, a licensing company for brands of toys, food and health products, a book publishing company and a production house for perfoming arts and concerts... etc. In addition, I also hope that since I am a huge Disney fan, it would be a great blessing if I could be appointed as a permanent global honorary ambassador of Disneyland.

Although there is a fire in everyone's heart, it can be bright and weak, but it can never be extinguished. Because dreams are the source of survival. Whether you can achieve your goals requires long-term efforts and persistence. As for the rest of my life, I will leave it to God to let nature take its course. I believe that if you are full of positive energy, simplify your life, be content and satisfied, and do not harm others or yourself, you will definitely get better and better.

Finally, I hope that with the love and support of readers, I can continue to publish albums of word songs with different themes to share my, your and other's life attitudes, unforgettable experiences and touching stories.

GAWAN

書名 Book Album Title：處子 VIRGIN
作者 Author：基宏 Gawan

官方網頁 Official Website: www.icongawan.com
Facebook/Instalgram/Twitter: IconGawan
小紅書：基宏
Linkedin: Gawan Lo
Youtube 頻道 Channel（文曲視頻 Word Song Videos）：Icon Gawan
電郵 E-mail: icongawan@gmail.com

出版 Publisher：超媒體出版有限公司 Systech Technology & Publications Limited
地址 Address：荃灣柴灣角街 34-36 號萬達來工業中心 21 樓 2 室
          Flat 2, 21/F., Million Fortune Industrial Centre,
          34-36 Chai Wan Kok St, Tsuen Wan, Hong Kong
電話 Tel：(+852) 3596 4296
傳真 Fax：(+852) 3003 3037
電郵 E-mail: info@easy-publish.org
網頁 Website: www.easy-publishing.org
香港總經銷 Hong Kong Distributor：聯合新零售（香港）有限公司
                        SUP Retail (Hong Kong) Limited

出版日期 Published Date：2024 年 7 月 / July 2024
圖書分類 Book Category：流行讀文、生活文化
                      Popular Reading Article, Lifestyle and Culture
國際書號 ISBN：978-988-8839-77-3
價目 Price：港幣 HKD$199

*2024 Production Right & Copyright Owned By Gawan Lo & Gawan Arts & Productions

All Rights Are Reserved

香港印刷及出版 Printed & published in Hong Kong

精裝書版本
HARDCOVER BOOK VERSION
收錄23首文曲
23 Word Songs Included

01 我在征服世人的狂痴　　01 I am conquering the craziness of the secular world
02 主禱者　　02 Prayer of god
03 默契　　03 Tacit
04 一對Converse的思念　　04 Missing of a pair of converse
05 熱帶雨　　05 Wet Season
06 脫節　　06 Out of touch
07 萬花筒　　07 Kaleidoscope
08 自甘墮落　　08 Be willing to fall
09 我我　　09 Me me
10 不請我 是你的損失　　10 Don't employ me Is your loss
11 心很痛 真的很痛　　11 Heart hurts Really hurts
12 戰爭　　12 Wars
13 遐想　　13 Reverie
14 來看一場周杰倫的演唱會　　14 Let's see a concert by Jay Chou
15 造愛後人類感傷　　15 Humans are sad after lovemaking
16 原色　　16 Original colour
17 究竟得不得到你的愛　　17 Can I exactly get your love
18 Free me　　18 Free me
19 少年得志...大不幸　　19 Misfortunate for being good and lucky…at young age
20 Goodbye song　　20 Goodbye song
21 偽人　　21 Hypocrite
22 Free Me (Piano version)　　22 Free me (Piano version)
23 年青無罪　　23 Young is innocent

基宏最初回實驗性文曲書本專輯
GAWAN 1ST EXPERIMENTAL WORD SONG BOOK ALBUM

WHO'S THAT VIRGIN ?
HE IS.... GAWANLO
1ST BOOK ALBUM

600本限量珍藏精裝書版本 附送4張精細圖片文字卡 售完即止
600 Limited Hardcopy Books Inclusive Of 4 Mini Bonus Photo Word Cards While Stocks Last

中英日韓四言對照　In 4 languages all-in-one: Chinese, English, Japanese and Korean

訂購請參閱基宏官方網站
To order, please refer to the official website of GAWAN
www.icongawan.com

Gawan 基宏
Presents 呈獻

百變 梅 艷芳
Anita Mui

The Legend Of The Pop Queen ~ Part I

中英對照 In English & Chinese languages
精裝書版本、電子書版本 (PUBU / AMAZON KINDLE) 同步上市
Hardcover Version & E-Book Version (PUBU / AMAZON KINDLE) are on sales

訂購請參閱基宏官方網站
To order, please refer to the official website of GAWAN
www.icongawan.com

繼鄧麗君之後，全球華人女歌手就是梅艷芳獨領天下！她不只是樂壇天后及影后，都早已在1980年代升格為無性別的全球華人天皇巨星，與譚詠麟和張國榮看齊。每一個百變形象、每一首經典金曲、每一部精彩電影和每一個輝煌成就，都一一紀錄。基宏籌備了20多年，是時候芳華綻放......此圖書榮獲日本EPSON 彩色影像大賞2006香港區評審特別獎。

After Teresa Teng, Anita Mui is the No.1 female Chinese singer in the world! She is not only the Queen of Pop and the Best Actress, but she has already been promoted to a genderless global Chinese superstar in the 1980s, on par with Alan Tam and Leslie Cheung. Every ever-changing image, every classic golden song, every spectacular movie and every brilliant achievement, all are recorded. GAWAN has been in preparation for more than 20 years, it's time for this book to bloom.... This book won the Japan EPSON Color Imaging Contest 2006 Hong Kong Jury Special Award.